DEFIANCE ON INDIAN CREEK

Praise for Defiance on Indian Creek

"*Defiance on Indian Creek* transports readers to the days of the American Revolution to follow the heart-stirring story of young Mary Shirley, who struggles to find her place in a turbulent world." —Charlene Whitman, author of *The Front Range* series

"...**Mary is a fun protagonist to follow** as the story progresses, because Still is able to give the reader the feeling of anguish from the girl and her struggles over choosing to place trust in her father and the lack thereof." —Literary Titan

"*Defiance on Indian Creek* **is a solid story**...While Mary is the storyteller here, there are strong male characters that young boys can relate to. Recommended for young readers on up." —James Fisher

"**Excellent for anyone teaching history through literature**. Defiance on Indian Creek fills an important gap because most revolutionary war historical fiction is written from the perspective of those living in New England."—Homeschool Teacher

"**Great historical fiction novel.** I collaborate with the social studies teacher locating books that teach reading comprehension and give students a better picture of life during certain time periods. This book is perfect for that."—Language Arts Teacher

BOOKS BY PHYLLIS A. STILL

Dangerous Loyalties Series
Defiance on Indian Creek, Book One
Fleeing the Shadows, Book Two
Warrior on the Western Waters, Book Three

Palisades of the Heart, Book Four

To the descendants of the brave men, women, and children mentioned in this historical fictional account. Be strong!

Defiance on Indian Creek

Dangerous Loyalties Book One

Phyllis A. Still

Climbing Tree Publications

DEFIANCE ON INDIAN CREEK

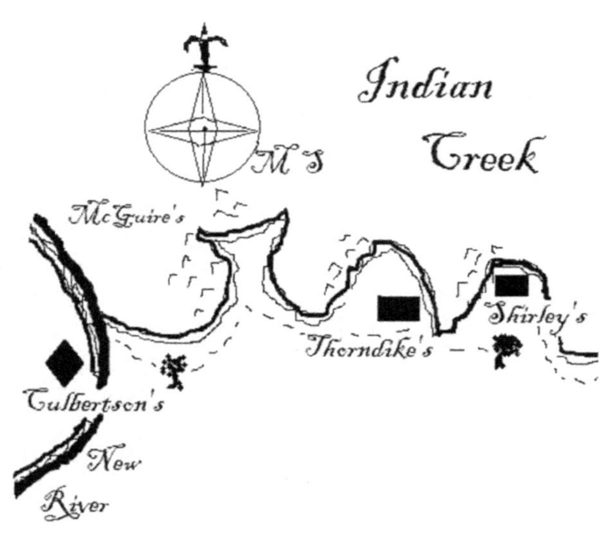
Indian
Creek
M's
McGuire's
Shirley's
Thorndike's
Culbertson's
New
River

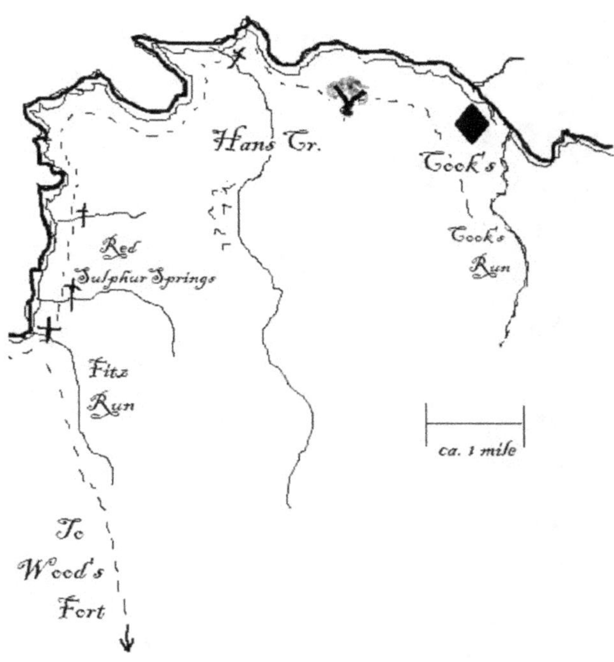

Hans Cr.
Cook's
Cook's
Run
Red
Sulphur Springs
Fitz
Run
To
Wood's
Fort
ca. 1 mile

Chapter One

Western Virginia, 1774

I weaved the gold embroidery thread into the last swoop of my letter *M,* laid the white neckerchief in my lap, then stared at Momma in the hazy glow of the hearth, and sighed. "It's been three weeks since George and I saw the Indian tracks. I'm tired of being cooped up and scared. Please, let us check for signs and hunt."

"I'll get the traps ready." My little brother leapt to his feet, letting his slate bang on the table where we sat. He smoothed his loose black hair behind his ears, retrieved his hat from its peg near the door, and waited.

Seated on the other side of the table, my younger sisters, Katie and Lizzy, glanced up from their needlework, wide-eyed.

Momma continued to stir the steamy pot of squirrel stew, then shook her head, and wiped sweat from her brow. "One more week. If Papa isn't home by next Sunday—we'll risk it."

Thoughts of Papa being among those wounded or dead at the Point made my eyes water. *Why else be delayed?* We'd learned of the mid-October ambush and the later peace treaty from our closest neighbor, Mr. Thorndike. He said that the men would be home the early part of November. "Papa should have been home two weeks ago. What if he's—"

Momma raised her eyebrows, tilting her head toward the youngest children playing on the board floor. Susie frowned, looking up from her pile of wooden clothespins and scraps of cloth. Nancy pooched out her lip, and Charlie let his block tower topple as he stared at the door.

"Papa?" Charlie asked.

I focused on the dried chamomile flowers that hung from the lower log beam to prevent my eyes from watering, then took a deep breath. "We need to get meat in the smokehouse. Papa would say so."

Momma's jaw clenched as her eyes narrowed.

I glanced at my hands. "I'm sorry. I didn't mean to sass."

Momma sighed. "Take Drummer and scout around the creek for Indian signs. But if he so much as bristles his fur, get back here quick. If you find nothing, traps can be set in the morning."

"And me?" George headed to the gun rack above the door.

Momma shook her head. "I won't risk both of you. Mary is the eldest and a better shot. You'll stand guard here."

His chest rose and fell in a quiet huff.

My heart raced as I dropped the almost completed neckerchief into the sewing basket and hurried to the door. I donned my sage-green knitted bonnet and gray wool coat, then shouldered the powder horn and leather-encased pine cartridge box. George handed me one of the two loaded flintlock rifles that were slightly longer than his height of forty inches, but a foot shorter than me.

Momma stepped up and wrapped me in her arms. Her breaths were shallow. "I'll try not to worry. Be safe."

I nodded. "I'll hurry, but if I have a shot at small game, I'll take it."

The black iron hinges creaked as I opened the oak plank door to a cold wind and squinted at the bright, clear afternoon.

"Be safe," echoed my siblings as Momma closed and latched the door behind me.

Drummer scrambled from under the porch and shook the dirt from his brown-and-white fur before sitting at my feet. I rubbed his head, stalling to calm my racing heart. With a deep breath, I forced my first steps. "Let's go, boy." I tapped my right leg, and Drummer heeled.

The woods were eerily quiet except for the occasional creaking of tree branches and crows alerting one another of our intrusion while we crunched on leaves of gold, brown, orange, and red. As we neared the creek, I slowed to examine the bushes for broken twigs and the ground for prints. Outside of the normal tracks of squirrel, deer, and coons, there was nothing alarming—until a gobble on the other side of Indian Creek made my blood run cold.

Indians imitate turkeys. I squatted among a tangle of vines and planted my right knee into the damp leaves, prepared to shoot. Drummer stood alert, sniffing the air. I pursed my lips to prevent foggy breaths from giving me away, just in case.

Something large rustled the leaves across the creek and flushed a crow from an oak tree. Its ruckus of caws echoed through the forest, and my heart raced. *Too late to run.* Drummer snarled with bristled fur and pulled his ears back. "Shh," I whispered to him

He sat but grumbled. I pulled the hammer back on the flintlock, filled the flash pan, then watched the darkening woods, ignoring the trickle from my nose.

Drummer sprang to his feet, growling, as the silhouette of a man ducked behind a sycamore tree. I gasped. *It is an Indian.*

I snapped my fingers, and Drummer hushed. Shallow breaths squeezed from my chest. *If I don't shoot, he'll scalp me.* I swallowed. My stomach churned. *God, help me.* I propped my elbow on my left leg, raised the stock to my shoulder, and aimed toward the tree. As a head eased into my sight, I held my breath, steadied the swaying barrel, and fired.

The flash stung my cheek. My ears crackled. Smoke burned my eyes and made me cough. With trembling hands, I pulled a paper cartridge from the box, bit off the tip, and poured the contents down the barrel. I slid out the rod, tamped wadding and bullet down the barrel, sucked in a deep breath, and prepared for a second shot.

A familiar whistle made my heart leap. Drummer wagged his tail and raced through the leaves toward the creek. I ran to the bank, weeping, and shouting, "Papa."

He emerged from behind the tree, holding a blood-soaked rag to his head with one hand while carrying his long-barreled rifle and beaver-skin hat in the other. *Oh no! I shot Papa.*

As he teetered across the boulders, my legs buckled, my ears roared like rushing water, and I landed on my rear, dropping the weapon. Papa said, "Mary" from a distant place before things went dark.

Rank body odor revived me in his arms, safe and warm, with glistening eyes scanning mine. "Take a deep breath." He stroked my head. "You're in shock."

I sucked in air and tried to sit.

"Steady now." He helped me.

Blood trickled from an inch-long cut on his forehead. Sobs rose from my belly. "I...shot you?"

"No, but you got that tree, and the bark found my head. It's just a graze. That blame turkey startled me. The next thing I knew, my foot slipped on a pile of leaves. Thankfully, I heard Drummer's growl and ducked. But I swallowed my sprig of mint—made it hard to whistle. Now, I know I should have waited."

"I thought you were an Indian because of the gobble and because you jumped behind that tree. Then your head moved out."

He nodded. "I understand your fear, little polliwog, but take a few seconds to see your target clearly, and make your shot sure. Thankfully, God has preserved us both today. I'm sorry."

His cheeks were chapped from a recent shave, and minty breath identified the speck of green in his teeth. His long black hair hung in a tidy braid down his back and made me smile. *He's cleaned up for Momma, but his coat smells horrible.*

He dabbed his wound before securing the rag in place over it with his hat. "Shall we go home to Momma now?"

As he pulled me to my feet, the sight of a bloodstain on the front of his coat gripped my throat. "Were you wounded in the battle?"

He glanced down, frowning. "No, not my blood. It stained before I could wash it out."

I wrapped my arms around his neck. "I'm glad you're home safe."

"Me too." He held me a minute, then stepped back. "What are you doing out here alone?"

My cheeks grew hot. "George and I saw moccasin tracks around the creek three weeks ago. Momma's been afraid to let us leave the yard since, but I convinced her to let me scout this afternoon. George wanted to come, but Momma made him stand guard at the window."

Papa hugged me to his chest. "Thank God the Indians are calming down and making peace again."

His good news made my belly flutter. "Maybe more families will settle along Indian Creek with girls my age. It would be fun to go to socials."

He grinned and shrugged. "Maybe so."

His lack of enthusiasm bothered me. "Don't you want more people to survey for? Wouldn't Momma enjoy a meetinghouse nearby for divine services? And how will I have suitors someday without socials? I'm making a special neckerchief to wear."

His brows kinked, and his jaw dropped. "You're only twelve. Why are you thinking about suitors?"

The shock in his voice made me chuckle. "I'll be thirteen in three months. But don't worry—I just want to be seen."

He laughed and shook his head, then secured his pack, rifle, and two clunky wooden canteens on his shoulder.

"Let's get home. I'm starving." He knelt and rubbed Drummer's neck. "Good boy. Come." Drummer leapt into a run but stopped to pee on a bush before circling us twice and heeling beside Papa.

When I lifted the gun barrel from the ground, an image of Papa staggering out with a bloody forehead flashed before my eyes. Tears pooled, but I blinked them away and slipped my trembling hand into his. He gave it a gentle squeeze.

Leaves crunched as we walked along the wooded path.

"How is everyone?" he asked

"All is well except ol' Aesop. He died on the way back from Mr. Thorndike's after delivering tobacco. We dragged him off the road as far as Little Sis would allow. Nothing left of him now."

He sighed. "Well, he was an old mule, but I'll have to barter a new one soon. Glad I didn't take Little Sis, but I sure missed riding my own mare." He stopped before reaching the yard and darted behind a pin oak tree, peeking around with an ornery grin. "Don't let on that I'm home. Go inside and pretend to be sad."

Irritation swept over me. The family would have heard the blast. *How can I explain without at least a rabbit in hand? Once he steps inside, they'll know I shot him.*

When I saw puffs of smoke meandering from the gray stone chimney of our two-story log cabin, I paused to breathe in the comforting scent of hickory. The dread of going inside made my stomach flutter and my heart race. The family would be excited to see Papa, but then they'd learn of his head wound.

Exhaling a deep breath, I approached the cabin. A shutter eased back from the paneless window, and butterscotch-tinted curtains flapped in the breeze. George's head poked out briefly before he flung open the door. "We heard a gunshot, and Momma about fainted."

I swallowed and stepped under the bark-shingled roof of the porch. "Accident. No Indians though."

"Not even a rabbit?" He frowned and stepped back from my glare, grunting, "Hmph."

The instant warmth inside and the hearty scent of stew soothed my jitters until I glimpsed Papa sneaking into the yard as I closed the door. My belly fluttered as I hung the rifle above the door. An iron lid clunked on the pot from the hearth as I turned toward my family. Sheer resolve kept me from spoiling Papa's surprise.

Momma stood before me with watery eyes, her oval face drawn and pale. She pulled me into her arms. "Thank God you're safe. That shot took ten years off my life."

"I'm sorry." I sighed, thinking of what almost happened.

She stepped back with a weak smile and kissed my cheek. "You and George may set out traps in the morning. Time to get supper now." As she turned back to the hearth, I noticed how tired and sad she seemed. Knowing how happy she was about to be made me smile.

Four-year-old Nancy hugged my waist. "Were you scared?"

"Yes." I knelt to hug her, then noticed Lizzy and Susie were dabbing their eyes as they gathered plates and forks for the table. It pleased me to know my siblings cared about me. Even Katie's eyes glistened, but she quickly turned toward the loft ladder when I glanced her way. She seemed to resent me most of the time.

A creak from the door made my breath catch. I watched it open bit by bit, before suddenly flying open with Papa standing in the threshold with a huge grin.

"How about venison jerky?" He propped his gun against the wall, dropped his gear on the floor with a thud, and held out his arms.

Momma squealed, flung her potholders on the board floor, then sidestepped Charlie, who was making a beeline to Papa. She squeezed in before him and wrapped her arms around Papa's neck, snuggling and heaving sobs. He spoke something in her ear that made her smile. His hands followed the contour of her back and cupped the roundness of her rump. I grinned. *She didn't notice his wound.*

When Momma stepped back, Papa turned to the younger children, motioning for them to come. Susie, Nancy, and Charlie swarmed his legs. Katie and Lizzy pried their way in next. My throat tightened. *One inch to the right and he wouldn't be here.* I blinked several times to keep tears away and plopped into the nearest chair at the table, thanking God for my bad aim.

George smiled and waited for an opening. After a quick hug, he stepped back. "Is that dried blood on your coat? Did you kill Indians?"

Papa sighed. "I'll tell you about it later."

"Yes, sir." He hung his head, then lifted Papa's rifle up to the rack.

Papa glanced at me and sighed. While holding the blood-soaked cloth in place, he easing the round brimmed hat from his head.

Tears defiantly pooled and trickled down my cheeks.

Momma gasped at the oozing wound and rushed to him with a clean rag. "What happened?"

I sighed and lowered my head.

"Shrapnel from a tree. It's not serious."

George turned to me, frowning. "You shot at Papa?"

I buried my face in my apron, sniffling, while Papa explained.

"Come now." Momma tapped my shoulder and took my hand, pulling me to my feet and into her arms. "His wound will heal, and you're both home safe. Come and stir the stew, please." She kissed my cheek and then went to Papa.

Wiping my face, I went to the fireplace and lifted the hot lid with long-handled tongs.

George stepped beside me, holding his palms toward the fire. "Can't believe you almost shot Papa," he whispered.

The taunt hurt. I shook the dripping ladle near his face. "Leave me be, or I'll smack you."

He sat hard, scooting away from my reach, and I returned to stirring. Sensing the stares of my family, I took a deep breath and faced them, uttering the expected apology. "I'm sorry for my outburst." I wasn't, really. At least not yet.

George stared at the floor as he went to the door. "I'll bring in more wood."

I turned back to the fire, still seething.

Seven-month-old Sally whimpered from the crib. I glimpsed Papa cuddle her to his chest. "Hi, baby girl, I'm your papa." He spoke in soft, high pitches. Sally stroked his scruffy face and giggled.

"There have been a lot of changes since August." He glanced at Momma with glistening eyes.

My gut wrenched at his sudden frown and the realization that being away from us bothered him.

Momma went to him, rubbing his shoulders. "You're home now, and all is well."

His smile returned as he hummed a German lullaby and carried Sally to his chair at the table.

I wiped my cheeks and met George coming in with an armload of firewood. "Sorry for my anger. But please don't tease me about shooting Papa again. It was terrible, and I thought he was an Indian."

He nodded and dropped the logs in the wood box near the hearth.

I drew a deep breath, thankful that I hadn't killed Papa or smacked George with the ladle.

The cabin filled with a flurry of clattering tin plates and wooden cups as Susie, Nancy, and Charlie set the table, giggling. Katie transferred the baby from Papa to her highchair, and Lizzy filled cups with water from the bucket.

Oak benches scraped the floor as we sat. Papa held Momma's chair for her before taking his place at the head of the table and bowing his head. My head seemed to float with the rise and fall of his deep, melodious voice in prayer, until he cracked with emotion. "God...save the king...and these colonies...Amen." He cleared his throat and grimaced. "Sorry. My mind is troubled a bit. Good men and God are trying to prevent a war with Britain. Much prayer is needed."

My jaw dropped. "Is it still about stamps and taxes?"

Momma frowned. "Nothing we need to worry about tonight."

Papa gave me a nod before scooping a spoonful of stew to his lips and slurping. He swallowed, then grinned at Momma. "Squirrel stew sure tastes better from your hearth."

Her face turned red.

His smile fell into a straight line. "I hear we're in need of a new mule?"

"Yes, the poor ol' thing." She winced. "But at least he lasted through hauling four hogsheads of tobacco to Mr. Thorndike's place."

"Well done. What price?"

Momma sat tall and beamed. "Stood my ground for eight pounds sterling per hogshead, even though Mr. Thorndike insists the value has fallen below seven. The inspector deemed it all good quality, so he relented. But he says tobacco won't be worth planting this spring because imports have stopped. Is he correct?"

My breath caught. *She didn't mention this before.*

Papa's brow furrowed. "I'll see him about it."

When Papa finished his stew, he leaned back, patted his stomach, and belched. Giggles traveled around the table.

George straightened in his chair, pushing his bowl aside. "May we please hear about the battle at the Point now?"

"Not tonight, son. I'm too weary." He sighed. "At least we don't have to worry about Shawnee raids. They've been pushed back across the Ohio. Now, we need level heads in Williamsburg."

"Time for bed, children." Momma stood, wiping Sally's messy face.

"We'll set traps in the morning," Papa said. "There's a wild turkey roaming the woods around the creek that I mean to be Christmas Eve supper."

I blurted, "Amen," but something about his use of "at least" made me cringe. With the Indian trouble over, and Papa home, life should be happy again. New settlers could come, and meeting houses would replace the need for blockhouses and forts. There should be socials and, hopefully, girls my age. *Why has Papa brought home such foreboding?*

Chapter Two

The afternoon sun streamed through the closed shutters while I mended my brown woolen petticoat that got snagged in the shrubs yesterday. A blustery wind seeped through and made the golden light of the tallow candle dance on the table, and I imagined a handsome man twirling me at a social.

Lizzy chuckled. "Why are you smiling at the candle like that?"

"Just thinking." I shook my head, then snipped the thread off the last stitch and tossed the hem toward the floor with a sigh. *Papa won't let me have suitors until I'm fifteen, anyway.*

The frantic gobbles of a turkey sent me scrambling outside with Momma and my sisters.

"Hullo," George shouted and waved as he emerged from the creek trail.

I squealed and clapped my hands at the sight of Papa holding the distressed fowl by its feet as he came into the yard. Whether it was the same bird that caused me to shoot at Papa or not, it pleased me to think so.

"Get the cage," Papa said.

Katie and I sprinted to the barn. The large cage was made of river cane with four sides and a top, but no bottom. The fibers on the cane pricked my hands as we lifted it from the pegs on the wall and carried it out of the barn.

"I hope Momma makes dressing without sage," Katie said.

"What?" I frowned. "It won't taste good without sage."

She wiggled her head at me. "Well, I don't like it, and I'm going to ask her to leave it out."

I ignored her challenge. She could irritate me on just about any topic, as if to prove herself my equal, often quipping, "You're only sixteen months older," as if it mattered.

Lizzy brought over a leather water pouch, and Momma mixed a little into a pan of milled corn. Papa set the turkey in the cage, latched the top, and hung the pouch on the outside to drip. George secured the cage to the ground with curved stakes. The bird panted, then pecked at the water. Momma offered it the mush, but the silly thing squawked, flapped its wings, and cowered in the corner.

"It will calm down once we leave," Momma said. "Should be good and plump in a few weeks for Christmas."

Katie stepped in front of me. "Can we please have dressing without sage?"

I almost shoved her.

Momma leaned her head back and chuckled. "No, but I can use a little less. It's not dressing without sage."

I smirked at Katie and followed Momma inside.

After supper, we gathered near the hearth and huddled on the floor around Papa's chair. I hugged my legs to my chest, anticipating his exciting story.

He closed his eyes a moment, then looked at Momma. Her rocker squeaked with a slow rhythm as she nursed Sally and nodded. "Mind you don't scare the little ones."

Nancy snuggled closer to Susie, proclaiming, "I'm not scared; I'm four." Susie held her hand.

Papa nodded and began in a calm manner. "I volunteered as a scout with William Fleming's company, under Colonel Lewis. We hacked through 160 miles of thick brush before reaching the junction of the Kanawha and Ohio Rivers. But we emerged into what seemed like a fairy-tale land with flaming red and golden leaves falling all around us. We named the place Camp Pleasant."

I pictured the place he described and felt its calmness—until his tone turned serious.

"For three days, we scouted a fifteen-mile radius for signs of Indians and waited for Governor Dunmore's regiment. Satisfied that the area was secure, we enjoyed a Sunday evening service. Upon retiring to my tent, I snuggled under my wool blanket at peace with the Lord."

Papa leaned forward, peering at us. "Momma won't let me say what came out of my mouth when the drummers beat to arms, jarring me from a sound sleep before daylight."

"Why won't Momma let you say?" Susie interrupted, staring at Momma.

"Because it wasn't nice. Now hush." George scowled.

Susie pouted. Papa raised his eyebrows at George, then winked at Momma. "She has to keep me nice. Now, where was I?"

"The Indians were attacking," I said.

He stared at the floor before glancing at us with a sigh. The intensity in his eyes made my skin prickle, and I gripped my legs tighter.

"Whoops and shouts erupted from the woods. I steadied my nerves, grabbed my gun, and scrambled out of the tent without my shoes—racing toward the river with the rest of my company. We ran up the riverbank to the left as another unit veered to the right. Seconds later, hundreds of shots crackled in the air. We rushed into a fray of swarming Shawnee warriors."

His eyes darted as he slowed his words, and I rocked, holding my breath.

"I hunched down, slowed my pace, and narrowed my aim in front of me, choking on the thick smoke that burned my eyes. When I knelt to reload, a tomahawk whirled past my left ear and thumped into a tree behind me. A screaming brave leapt at me with a scalping knife. I jabbed my bayonet into his belly and shoved him away as another warrior lunged, but someone shot him in the back." Papa shook his head. "He fell against me—that's whose blood is on my coat."

Papa stood, wiping his sweaty brow on the way to the door. He flung it open to a quick blast of cold air.

"That's enough," Momma said. "Papa should rest."

"But where did the Indians come from?" George asked.

Her double clap made me jump with her command, "Hush now."

"No, it's fine." Papa closed the door and returned to his seat. "I need to talk about it, and the children need to hear how horrible war is. They may be facing it sooner than later."

I swallowed the lump in my throat. "What do you mean?"

"I hope nothing, so long as Cornstalk keeps his word to stay neutral."

Fear of new raids knotted my stomach. Momma looked pale.

Papa reached for her hand and mouthed, "Sorry," then turned to George. "The Shawnee were twenty miles downriver, watching us scout and waiting until dark to cross. If not for divine providence, they would have scalped us in our sleep. A lone hunter rushed into camp, shrieking the alarm that woke our drummer.

"Several times during the harrowing battle at the river, the braves fell back in retreat, but an ear-piercing command from Chief Cornstalk rallied them and made the hair on the back of my neck prickle. Sounded something like 'Oui-shi-cat-to-oui, oui-shi-cat-to-oui.'"

Papa's shout sent a tingle up my back, and Charlie scurried into my lap with a whimper.

Momma shot out of her chair. "That's enough. The little ones need to go to bed now." She swayed to soothe the startled baby.

With a sheepish grin, he whispered, "Sorry, I got carried away. But it means 'be strong'—like in the story of Joshua." Excitement beamed from his eyes. "The older children can stay a while longer."

"I'm not a little one anymore, am I, Momma?" Suzie tried to sound grown-up.

"Me either." Nancy stood in protest.

"Bedtime for everyone under seven," Momma said.

Papa hugged them all good night before I carried Charlie to his straw-stuffed pallet on the floor beside Momma and Papa's bed. He pulled his brown wool blanket around his shoulders, and I kissed his soft cheek, whispering, "Night-night. Be strong." Charlie hugged my neck and turned toward the wall.

As I returned to my place, an image of Papa dressed as the biblical Joshua standing on the bank of the Jordan River shouting, "Oui-shi-cat-to-oui" made me chuckle.

Momma returned to her rocker, eyeing Papa. "Keep your voice down, please."

He nodded. "About sundown, the Indians disappeared across the river."

George slapped his leg. "You mean they got away?"

"Yes, and Cornstalk negotiated a treaty with Governor Dunmore. That's when the morale of the men turned ugly. Many demanded an attack on the Shawnee villages across the Ohio, but General Lewis maintained discipline." He sighed. "Suspicious fellows are accusing the governor of sending us into an ambush. Tempers have flared. Men are rallying for independent militias, and some are proposing a continental army."

He sat back in his chair, staring at Momma. Momma took a deep breath, and mine caught. *Will he have to leave again?*

"There's going to be a land rush for Kentucky territory now that the border is secure. Blockhouses are being fortified all along the Clinch River to ensure peace with the Indians."

I frowned. *What does Kentucky have to do with anything?*

Papa stroked his chin, and my heart skipped a beat. Chin-stroking meant he wanted Momma's approval for something. I looked at Momma. Her eyes narrowed as if warning him to hush, but he didn't.

"They say the land is fertile, teaming with game, and surveyors will be in high demand. If war breaks out, we'll be safer in Kentucky. I don't want to fight His Majesty's Royal Army."

The words jumbled in my head. *He wants us to move.*

Momma shook her head and stood. Her eyes darted as she spoke. "It's too dangerous. Why risk our lives because of the actions of fool-hearted men? It's bedtime, children." She averted her eyes and rushed to the back corner, sobbing.

My jaw dropped. She had never been so defiant, at least not in our hearing, although she and Papa did have loud discussions in the barn sometimes.

He stared at the fire another minute before standing with a sigh and retrieving his pipe from the mantle. "I'm going to check on the livestock and have a smoke on the porch."

Katie and Lizzy kissed his cheek, then climbed the ladder to the loft. George shrugged and followed them, but I lingered. Papa eased the door shut.

Momma emerged from the corner, sniffling, as she grabbed her shawl and headed out the door with a faint, "I need to speak to Papa alone."

I climbed the ladder in a stupor. We just settled here in March and endured the Indian raids. *Why flee now?*

The milder weather through December allowed Papa and George to set traps and hunt each morning. Soon our smokehouse held an abundance of plump venison, boar, and small game. My hands were still chapped from all the salting of meat.

But a cold northerly wind wrestled the door as I held it open for George after supper. The scent of smoky venison from the smokehouse followed him inside and blended with the lingering aroma of our devoured Christmas Eve turkey. He peered over his armload of firewood, grinning as he stamped slushy snow from his boots on the porch. "Thank you."

My sisters had finished drying the dishes, and Papa was seated in his chair near the hearth, holding his large

German Bible, ready to read the traditional Bethlehem story.

Since his return from the Point, he'd seemed distracted and distant. Like now, staring into the fire without flinching as George dropped logs into the wood box.

I sighed and sat cross-legged on the floor. Charlie settled beside me, and the others soon followed. Momma retrieved Sally.

Papa smiled and held his open Bible toward us, showing the first pages full of swirling pale-green vines, purple grapes, and ornate German lettering. Names, dates, and other notations filled perfectly straight-drawn lines.

"These are the names of your ancestors who risked death to accept the teachings of Martin Luther. They, and many others, fled their homes in the Rhineland, accepting the generous English king's offer to come to the colony, free to read this book as Protestants. Oaths of allegiance were sworn and signed by them." He closed the book and laid it in his lap. "I swore an oath of loyalty to His Majesty as a youth and again when I fought against the French. Breaking an oath is a serious matter, and I intend to keep mine. However, many of our neighbors rail against the king and wish him ill because he has been oppressive. But he needs our prayers for good sense, and I need your trust as the days grow evil around us."

"Of course we trust you, Papa," I said.

George looked at Papa. "What about Kentucky?"

Kentucky hadn't been mentioned since the day Momma followed Papa to the barn, and I assumed the matter had been settled.

Papa stroked his chin once, then lowered his hand and focused on Momma. "For now, we'll remain on Indian Creek as loyal subjects to His Majesty. But if independent militias form against the orders of the governor"—he faced Momma without flinching—"I will insist on the move."

Her eyes widened and her nostrils flared, but she turned toward the fire.

Why is he ruining our Christmas joy by speaking of these things? "May we hear the Christ story now?" Irritation flew from my mouth without thinking.

Papa focused on me, clearing his throat as he turned a few pages, and began reading in German.

But I couldn't pay attention. The world seemed to be ending, as mentioned in a Bible verse I couldn't remember. Something about wars and rumors of war.

Chapter Three

February 17, 1775

Creaking floorboards woke me as George crept past my pallet, whispering, "Happy birthday, Sister," then scurried down the ladder.

A quick glance at the loft shutters revealed the lack of light outside and diminished my hope for a clear day. The clatter of pans downstairs, the smell of sourdough baking and bacon frying, sent me flinging my covers aside. *Momma's baking my cake.* I found my sage-gray jacket and practical brown petticoat in the dim light and dressed.

Katie slunk past me and grabbed the horsehair brush first. She brushed her long black tresses and seemed to take her time on purpose. When I sighed, she glared.

Lizzy braided her hair without brushing first. Even in the shadows, strands of auburn hair poked from her head like porcupine quills.

I chuckled. "Would you like help with your hair?"

"Yes, please." She loosened the braid.

Katie slapped the brush into my waiting hand.

Pain shot up my arm. I wanted to smack her face. "Why are you so grumpy?"

She smirked and smoothed her hair back. "Happy birthday, but don't expect to get away with more bossing just because you're thirteen."

We exchanged scowls, and Lizzy stood back watching.

Momma hollered from below, "Are you girls coming down today?"

I narrowed my eyes at Katie one more time before answering. "Yes, ma'am. I'm helping Lizzy with her hair." Thirteen still felt like twelve.

Katie huffed, flipping her braid at me, and climbed down.

Lizzy pouted. "She needs Papa to take her to the barn for a good switching."

"Or a good dousing from the water bucket." I chuckled.

I kissed the top of her head when I finished tying sinew to the ends of her braid. "You look the most like Momma, I think."

She beamed. "Really?"

"Yes, and just as sweet, too."

"Thank you. Let's hurry down so I can give you my gift."

I smiled and followed her down the ladder into the dim room. "I can't wait to see."

"My big girl is thirteen—my, my. Come here and kiss my cheek." Momma's hands were busy removing my round birthday cake from the Dutch oven.

Birthday wishes echoed from Susie and Nancy as they decorated the table with twigs of pine and cedar. Twelve white candles were glowing around the wooden wreath, and the center candle was adorned with pebbles.

Charlie danced around me, repeating, "Appy burppy." I squatted to hug him and then went to Momma.

Her cheek was salty to my lips, like bacon splatters. "Shall I help with anything?"

"You may strain the coffee. Papa and George will be in soon."

As I strained pungent black liquid through cheesecloth, the cabin door swung open with a cool draft and a glimpse of the charcoal sky. George entered with kindling. "Helga just dropped her calf. Come see."

"Can we have milk now?" Susie asked.

Momma chuckled. "Not yet. The calf will get the early milk for three days."

"My first birthday gift." I smiled and followed my siblings into the musty barn.

The steaming brown-and-white calf staggered to its feet. Helga mooed, and the calf wobbled to her teats.

Nancy squealed and clapped her hands. "It's beautiful."

"She birthed a good, strong calf by herself." Papa came to me and kissed my forehead. "Happy birthday, little polliwog."

"Let's leave them alone now and get back inside before we catch our deaths." Momma shifted Sally on her hip and took Charlie's hand. "Breakfast is ready, and we have celebrating to do."

When I finished the last bite of my honey-sweetened cake, Papa stood with his cup in the air, grinning. "Now, I borrow a custom from our Irish neighbors and pronounce a birthday blessing for my grown daughter. May the path before you be made clear, may you feel God's breath as he whispers in your ear, may your fear be turned into strength, may your weeping be turned into joy, and may your future be of great length."

His "grown daughter" pronouncement made me beam. I stood, raising my cup. "Thank you, Papa."

Nancy leapt from her chair. "May we give our gifts now?"

Momma nodded, and my siblings scurried about retrieving the items they had made. One at a time, they laid them before me, and I thanked them with hugs.

With a timid grin, Charlie gave me a round river rock.

George gave me a reed whistle. "Just in case you get lost while foraging."

Suzie had embroidered pink and yellow flowers on a linen handkerchief. "This is for when you get married someday."

Lizzy had knitted a pair of socks. "I hope they fit."

Momma surprised me with a new chemise. "It may be a little too big now, but not within the year." She glanced at my chest and winked.

My breath caught. *She noticed.* I had been too embarrassed to mention my swelling breasts.

Nancy beamed. "Momma, let me help." She pointed to a few jagged stitches along the hem.

With a little prompting, Sally blew me a kiss.

Then Katie approached, keeping her hands behind her back until she stood in front of me.

"I'm sorry about the brush." She brought her closed hands in front of her and crossed them. "Choose."

I tapped her left hand. She grinned and revealed nothing, but her other hand opened with knitted lace. She unraveled what seemed to be a half yard and gave it to me.

My grudge against her softened. I threw my arms around her in a hug before stepping back. "This is fine work. Thank you. I will save it in my hope box."

She seemed a bit startled. I smiled, and she blinked, pooling tears away.

Papa scooted my chair from the table and took my hand while I stood. He looked into my eyes with a sheepish grin. "Someday you'll dance with a suitor, but for the next three years, you'll dance with your family."

He burst into a German folk song, stamping around me in a dance called a polka. Momma danced with Charlie in her arms, and my siblings joined in. Laughter filled the cabin as we danced two polkas and one and a half Irish jigs.

Drummer's vicious barks in the yard interrupted. Papa parted the shutters, then looked at Momma. "It's Mr. Thorndike." He stepped onto the porch. "Stay inside." With a snap of Papa's finger, Drummer hushed and heeled.

Curious, I held the door ajar, tilting my head around him to see a chestnut mare cantering into the yard carrying our closest neighbor, Mr. Thorndike.

"Welcome, Henry." Papa waved and met him in the yard. Mr. Thorndike dismounted, scowling. He handed Papa what looked like a gazette and pointed to something in it. Papa shook his head.

"Close the door, Mary," Momma said. "You're letting in the cold, and it's bad manners to eavesdrop."

A sigh accompanied my compliance. "Appears to be bad news." I sat at the table watching the door.

Momma laid her hand on my shoulder. "We'll know soon enough. It's best to turn worry into prayer. Whatever is happening is God's knowing or doing, anyway. Ask for his help to endure it."

I closed my eyes and complained to him instead. *Why not just keep everyone happy and good?*

Katie bumped my arm with her elbow. I cut my eyes at her, then rose to help clear the table.

In another minute, Papa entered with his jaw clenched and laid the *Virginia Gazette* on the table. He released a deep breath and sat. "All imports to Britain have stopped, and tobacco prices have fallen to five pounds sterling per hogshead."

My heart sank. *What will we do?* I looked to Momma for a hopeful reaction, but she sat beside Papa, shaking her head.

Papa reached for her hand. "I'm going to join a road survey crew, which means I'll be gone days at a time. I'll barter the use of a couple of slaves, come May. No more than two days, just to make the mounds."

What? Back in March, when we left our place on the Shenandoah River, he said slaves were expensive and too much responsibility. Momma had argued that 527 acres would be too much for us to manage. But Papa made barters with other settlers for cabin building and clearing our first two acres. *Why not just ask the neighbors for help again?*

George beamed. "You mean we don't have to build tobacco mounds?"

How can he be so happy about slaves? I kicked his leg under the table.

He jerked his head toward me, glaring.

Papa continued. "No, but after we clear two new acres for the tobacco, you'll be plenty busy helping Momma plant and harvest while I'm gone." His face drooped in a frown as he turned to Momma. "We'll need an acre in corn to mill and one for seed. An acre garden should be manageable and provide what we need." He bit his lips and gazed at Momma. "Preserve as much as you can for the move to Kentucky in August. I know a young couple willing to live on the place for two years and pay the quit-rent fee. I'll grant them the claim if we stay in Kentucky."

I stared at him. His words sounded final. I shoved my chair away from the table and stood. "No, Papa. Why can't we stay here?" My eyes watered.

With a patient look, he patted the table in front of me. "Calm down and sit."

I plopped onto the bench with my siblings staring at me.

Momma rubbed her forehead and drew a deep breath.

Papa held up the *Gazette*, turning to the third page. "Our neighbors in Fincastle County have pledged love and loyalty to His Majesty. But only if he rescinds unconstitutional laws that have removed our liberties as British subjects; otherwise, they say this: 'We declare that we are deliberately and resolutely determined never to surrender them to any power on earth but at the expense of our lives.'"

He laid the paper aside, frowning. "Mr. Thorndike informs me of an upcoming freeholders' meeting for our county. Two delegates will be chosen to attend a secret convention in Richmond this March to hear the case against His Majesty. Lord Dunmore isn't invited since the first such meeting didn't meet with his approval. So, there you have it. War is imminent, and I want to be in Kentucky after the harvest."

"Oh, Michael, surely peace will hold." Momma shook her head, wiping tears from her cheeks.

"Pray that it will, but a well-preserved harvest won't go to waste, in either case. I'm going to Mr. Thorndike's now, to trade the seed bags we don't need for a new mule." He turned his attention to me. "I need you to head the seedbed digging today while I'm gone. It's a little dreary outside, but the clouds aren't drooping."

I crossed my arms and held my tongue. I wanted to call him a coward.

He raised his eyebrows, locking eyes on me until I lowered mine. "Yes, sir."

Still seething, I retrieved my winter moccasins, slathered them with a fresh layer of bear grease mixed with beeswax, and tightened the laces around my ankles. I followed my family into the cold, gloomy yard, sending a plea to God. *Please make Papa change his mind before August.*

Papa hitched Little Sis to the wagon and climbed into the seat. "Should be back in time for supper."

I waved out of habit and went into the barn for shovels.

Katie and George grabbed their own shovels and set to work, stabbing the blades into the soggy ground. I handed Lizzy the spade. "Take turns with Suzie and supervise Nancy and Charlie with the hand shovels."

I went to the opposite end and drove my spade into the mud, wiggling it to release the suction before dumping the heavy, dripping blob to the side. In a few minutes, I relaxed and glanced toward Momma.

She had placed Sally in the cart with a basket of wooden clothespins but had only dug a short distance. I took a break and watched the toddler giggle and toss the pins out one by one. I chuckled as Momma retrieved them thrice, then threw her hands up, laughing. "I'll be more productive inside." She smiled at me and pointed to an oak while lifting Sally to her hip. "The lunch basket is hanging on that limb there."

I nodded and went to check on my charges.

Nancy and Charlie were digging small holes as directed by Lizzy, and Susie made fine progress with the spade. "Good job, everyone. We'll work until the trenches meet and then take a break."

Once completed, we compared our blistered hands before plunging them into the cold spring water to soothe the throbbing.

We sat on logs, and I passed the basket of leftover hoecakes. "Now we have to drop in tobacco seeds and cover them with manure and straw."

"We should divide the jobs," George said. "I'll seed, you can shovel in dung, and Katie can lay the straw on top."

I stood, crossing my arms. "Katie will shovel the dung, you will cover it with straw, and I'll teach Lizzy, Susie, and Nancy how to seed. Papa left me in charge, and that's how it's going to be."

Katie glared and stomped toward the dung cart.

Once finished, we cleaned up in the spring. My sisters went in the cabin, and George went to the barn to rake out stalls.

I squatted down to pat Drummer, but he hopped up yapping at Papa and a braying mule.

Papa waved for me to come.

We entered the barn to a plume of hay dust and dirt that made me sneeze.

"Yippee." George hung the rake on the wall and joined us. "Can we name him Gideon? I like the story of Gideon."

Papa nodded. "Sounds like a fine name. We'll test him out now, hauling in fresh straw."

He unsaddled the mare and hung a bulging saddlebag on the peg, then handed me the horse brush. "Brush Little Sis for me, please."

He talked George through hitching Gideon to the cart while I brushed his mare's sweaty withers.

"We'll be back in a bit." Papa stepped out of the barn.

George tugged on the rope, and the mule followed, pulling the squeaking cart through the doorway.

My gaze drifted to the overstuffed saddlebag. With a final swipe down the mare's back, I eased toward the peg, watching the doorway while poking the bag with the brush. It fell onto a pile of clean hay, spilling paper packets of surveys and maps. My heart pounded as I secured the brush and pilfered through them. Prying into Papa's personal matters could lead to a sound scolding, but curiosity lured.

The surveys seemed to be of no consequence, except one bearing the diagram of a large *Y* in the center. Its midpoint bore a circled *MS*, which I knew to be Papa's initials on the big red oak tree in our front yard. The description under the plat read: "From said tree, westerly forty poles to a poplar tree marking the beginning of old Indian path, thence up same winding course three miles to Thorndike line, thence, six miles to weep no more for my Irish lad." *What does that mean? Six miles past Thorndike's place has to be the New River crossing near Fort Culbertson. But why the riddle?*

The squeaky wheels of the cart alerted me in time to refold the document, slip it into its paper sleeve, and stuff it into the bag. Papa caught me hanging it on the peg when he entered.

Sweat broke out on my forehead as I faced him with a partial confession. "I bumped your saddlebag with the brush and the surveys fell out. They landed on clean hay. I'm sorry." Guilt lingered.

He left George unhitching the cart and retrieved the bag. "Guess I better be more careful. These are important surveys." He peered inside and rearranged a few.

"Are they local?" My heart raced. I bit my lips, hoping I didn't give myself away.

His eyes widened as he searched mine. "Some are."

I looked at my feet; then boldness rose from my gut. "Are you going to Fort Culbertson for supplies soon?"

His face seemed to turn pale. "Why?"

My legs felt shaky. "I...I'd like to go."

He unclenched his jaw and beamed. "I'll think about it. I have a few surveys to do up that way for Cornelius McGuire at the end of March."

Afraid he would suspect my snooping if questioned further, I nodded and made a quick exit, piecing together the clues gained so far and growing more intrigued. I concluded that the McGuires were Irish and lived near Ft. Culbertson, at the six miles' point. The weeping part intrigued me, but I needed more information. Maybe one of the other surveys contained the answer.

I swallowed a sudden lump in my throat at the thought of sneaking another look. Then I repented of the wicked idea and entered the cabin, feeling older for the first time all day.

Chapter Four

That confounded riddle taunted me at least once every day. "Weep no more for my Irish lad" gave me a headache, even now. But Papa was leaving this morning on for a weeklong survey job for Cornelius McGuire, and said he wasn't going to Fort Culbertson.

I hurried down the ladder to help Momma with breakfast.

She smiled from her rocker and pointed to a pot simmering at the hearth. "There's corn porridge in the pot and some venison sausage in the warmer. Papa milked Helga before he left. He wanted to be at the McGuire's place by daybreak."

I felt a strange relief that he was gone, but missed hugging him goodbye.

Momma rose from the chair to set the table. "Wake your siblings, and we'll get an early start on the day. It's a frosty morning, but I think it will be a perfect wash day for sheets and doing some foraging. I need you to check the traps with George and bring home a basket full of wild violet blossoms. I want to be able to make cough syrup in Kentucky this winter. I'll leave a sheet on the barn ladder for a drying cloth."

"Yes, ma'am."

I would have preferred Katie accompany George, but she wasn't as good a shot if danger arose. Sometimes night predators found the trapped game and could be feasting on them when we arrived. Shouting would send most of them scurrying, but not a bobcat or bear.

Reaching the loft, I spoke in soft tones and tried not to sound bossy. "Breakfast is waiting. Momma wants to get an early start on laundry day, so please bring your sheets down." They stirred without complaint.

I gathered my bedding, then gave the warning "Look out below" as I tossed them to the floor and descended the ladder. I opened the door to a white frosted yard and dropped the sheets onto the porch.

There was a slower, peaceful pace to the morning with pleasant smiles and conversations around the table. Papa's absence seemed to lift the stresses of the last few months from my shoulders. All through March, we had chopped trees, dragged branches, and hauled rocks from the forest, clearing a new tobacco field. Growing only enough tobacco for personal use and seedpods seemed a futile waste of time to me, but I couldn't say so out loud.

We finally finished yesterday, in spite of a cold drizzling rain.

Momma rose from her chair first. "Well now, it's time to get busy."

I scooted my chair back and stood, glancing at George. He remained seated, crossed his arms on the table, and fixed his eyes on Momma. "May I check the traps by myself?"

Land sakes. I plopped back down, staring at him.

"I don't need help resetting them anymore, and Papa hasn't found any signs of Indians. Please?"

Momma wore a pleasant smile as if she were amused. "You may not. Nor shall you ask again until you're twelve, not eight."

"What if you encountered some wild thing or a roaming Indian?" The thought horrified me.

George's eyes rolled as he stood. "Well, I get to choose which way to go. Papa told me the best way."

Katie pulled his arm. "Help me hang the kettle first."

They went outside, followed by Lizzy and Susie racing to the spring to tote water.

"Too soon, a man." Momma sighed and sat in her rocker with Sally.

I shook my head. "Too small for Papa's shoes, anyway." I lifted the rifle from the rack and grabbed the basket. "I'll tether him if I have to."

As I met him in the yard, he pointed west. "This way."

"No. I need to gather violet blossoms first. Then we'll check the closest trap from there."

He sighed and lowered his head. "I knew you'd find a way to take over. Can I at least carry the rifle?"

I nodded. "Now hush and come with me. The meat has to be fresher than the blooms."

He followed me through the woods to the exact location of a prolific patch of violets under a large, old dogwood tree in full bloom. Its white canopy sparkled in the sunlight above a ground covering of sky-blue blossoms nesting in green, heart-shaped leaves. "Stand guard here while I pick."

"All right, but hurry." He scanned the area, then leaned against a sycamore tree, cradling the weapon in the crook of his arm.

I picked every blossom I could find, and within a few minutes, the half-peck basket was full. I smiled at George. "Now you may lead the way to the traps."

He stared at me, frowning. "I need to tell you something. But first you have to promise not to let on you know."

His serious face worried me. I held up my right hand. "I promise."

"When Papa and I were tending to the livestock in the barn two weeks ago, someone gave a double knock from the outside back corner. Papa told me to go on to the cabin. As I was leaving, I looked back and saw a man's arm slip through a loose board with a bundle of papers. Papa tucked them inside his coat. Well, I wanted to know what was going on, so I sneaked around back and listened."

I covered my mouth, surprised by his disobedience to Papa, but sympathized with his reason.

He glanced at his foot and rolled a pebble under his shoe before peering at me. "I couldn't make out what the other fellow said, but Papa asked if the willow was secure."

George paused. "You okay? Why are you holding your breath like that? Do you know what it means?"

I blew out the trapped breath. "I'm all right—just caught off guard. I don't understand it either." *Should I tell him about the riddle?* "It's all very strange. What did the man say?"

"I don't know. The leaves rustled. The man slunk away, and I ran to the cabin. But when Papa came inside, he wasn't wearing his coat anymore. What I can't figure out is why the man came on foot in the dark, and why Papa asked him about a willow tree? What do you think it means?"

I couldn't risk telling him what I knew. He would give something away, and I'd lose Papa's trust forever. That would be more devastating than his strap on my rear. "It's none of our business. And Papa will tan your hide if he catches you eavesdropping like that. Now, we need to tend to the traps."

George sighed and bobbed his head. "Remember, you promised not to tell."

I nodded and followed him through the woods to the first trap. A good-sized rabbit was caught by one leg and lay panting. I made George slit its throat because that part always made me squeamish. After that, it was food. I gutted, then tied its feet with sinew, and George draped it over a stick for easier carrying.

I thought about the survey clues as we journeyed up the ridge trail. A willow tree made sense with the weeping part of the riddle, which meant six miles near the New River crossing was a weeping willow tree. But why would someone pass documents to Papa through a loose board instead of riding into the yard and announcing himself properly? Why would the location of the willow tree need to be secure? Then a new question arose. What location lies on the northeastern arm of the *Y*?

My mind raced. Papa had mentioned a fort farther up Indian Creek named Cook's. The inclusion of the forts on Papa's survey plat gave me a sinking feeling that he was involved in scouting activities, which usually meant Indians. But why the secrecy, unless—my breath caught as Papa's words came back to me. *"The children need to know how terrible war is. They will be faced with it sooner or later."*

Papa wouldn't be involved in sedition. Uneasiness knotted my stomach. *But what is he doing? I need to find his documents.* My heart fluttered. *Just once more.*

We returned to the barn with two gray rabbits for the stew pot and a half-eaten red fox. George laid the carcasses on the butchering table, and I handed him the sharpest knife. "If you don't need help skinning, I'll get these petals laid out."

George shook his head as he sliced opened the fox's belly. "Naw, I can do it. Too bad her fur is damaged; she was a pretty one."

"It's enough for a cap or mittens, though." I lifted the linen cloth Momma left draped over the bottom rung of the ladder, placed it atop the basket, and climbed into the barn loft.

I unfurled the sheet toward the draft-free corner and dumped the faint-sweet-scented blossoms out to dry a few hours. As I turned to leave, something caught my eye in the corner rafters. I stepped back, craning my neck to see better. A wooden box was nestled almost out of sight, but I would need something to stand on to reach it. My stomach fluttered. *Could this be Papa's hiding place?*

The milking stool came to mind, but I couldn't fetch it without rousing George's curiosity.

At that moment, Katie yelled from the barn door. "Can you help me finish the washing? My arms are about to drop off. I'm on the last sheet."

"Coming." I gave the box a quick glance and descended the ladder, spying the stool on the way out.

Katie tossed a sheet into the kettle and tamped it down with the wooden paddle as I approached, then frowned. "What's wrong with Papa?"

I jerked my head in surprise. "What do you mean?"

"Why is he afraid to join the militia? Why do we have to go to Kentucky?"

I shrugged. "I've had the same questions."

Using a long stick, I helped Katie lift the hot dripping sheet from the kettle and placed it on the wash table before spreading it out. "But maybe he'll change his mind about loyalty to the king soon, and we won't have to leave."

I couldn't believe I was having such a conversation with Katie, and that she wasn't opposing me.

Katie rubbed a sliver of lye soap over the sheet. "Well, it's troubling me, and we're about to have slaves, too. Where will they sleep?"

My breath caught. "I forgot about slaves." Shock turned to sadness. "In the barn, I suppose. We barely have room for ourselves in the cabin."

"I'm going to pray extra hard for Papa to change his mind." Katie turned away, sniffling.

"Me too." *And I'm going to see what's in that box.*

We carried the sheet to a rinse barrel, took turns dunking it until it cooled, then transferred it to another barrel for the final rinse. Next, Katie lifted one end of the sheet from the water and backed away while I held onto the other end. Standing opposite of each other, we twisted out most of the water and carried to the clothesline.

"Thank you for helping." Katie smiled.

I nodded on my way back to the barn.

"These are finished." George held up the processed rabbits as I entered.

"Take them to Momma, please, and chop some firewood. I'll finish up in here."

His brow kinked as he studied me. "Why is firewood your concern?"

I had to think fast. I didn't want him coming back to the barn. "Well, it looks a little low, and we'll be moving the cooking outside soon."

He huffed and snatched the rabbits on his way out.

My heart raced as I snatched the three-legged stool and carried it up the ladder. I shoved the straw out of the way until the stool didn't wiggle before stepping up. I stared at the small rectangular chest a moment, weighing the consequences before sliding it from the beam and lowering it to the floor. My heart raced as I dragged the simple metal hook off the small peg and raised the hinged lid.

Several paper-sleeved packets lay inside. I squeezed the sides of each one to glimpse the contents, before finding the one with a *Y* and a description of the northeastern arm. This time, from Papa's oak tree, one had to take the eastern trail to the south bend of Indian Creek, then meander northerly 8.6 miles along the creek to a sharp southerly bend. From there it was four-tenths of a mile to a forked hickory tree marked *CS*. "So a rolling stone can gather no moss." I sighed and rolled my eyes at another dang riddle.

I flipped back through the other envelopes and found one that wasn't a survey, nor was it Papa's writing. It read: 'Proceed posthaste to Wood's. Establish contact and dispatch.' Signed with the initials *C.W.P.*

I growled. My desire to know what Papa was up to had tempted me to pry into affairs he wanted hidden. But why? I replaced the sleeves exactly the way I found them and hoisted the chest onto the rafters.

The forked tree grows near Fort Cook, but the riddle and the note only added more secrets. I rubbed my hand across the blossoms to turn them over, and then lifted the stool and climbed down.

Katie was standing in Helga's stall, petting the calf.

I stayed calm.

She faced me. "What were you doing up there?"

"Turning the flowers over." I averted my eyes, hoping she believed me.

"With the milking stool?"

"Well, I decided to sit and think a bit." My cheeks burned from the foolish-sounding excuse.

"You're lying. I see your face turning red." Her head bobbed toward the rafters. "And besides, I saw you put a box up there. What are you hiding?"

I couldn't tell her the truth about everything, but she needed to know the box wasn't mine. "I saw the box up there and wanted to know what was inside. It's just some of Papa's old surveys, so I put it back. Are you going to tell Papa I was snooping?"

Katie frowned. "Why would he be storing surveys up there and not in the cabin?"

"I'll let you ask him." I smiled, knowing she wouldn't dare.

Chapter Five

On the morning of April twenty-second, I rose before dawn with my stomach fluttering. I chose my sage-green petticoat, bright-yellow bodice, and the white neckerchief that showed off my swirling gold initials, which swooped into sprigs of green leaves at the end. Now I needed Momma's approval and help with my hair. I descended the ladder, hoping I didn't look as silly as I felt.

When Papa had returned from his survey job at the beginning of the month, he told about a Mr. Henderson's independent purchase of Kentucky land from the Cherokee. "He intends to sell claims cheap, without the king's quit-rent tax. Governor Dunmore and others are outraged. My friend Daniel Boone led the road crew that cleared the old buffalo trail over the Cumberland Mountains." He laughed. "The settlement will be called Boonesborough."

I had wanted to cover my ears, but he started talking about going to Fort Culbertson. "I need to trade furs for supplies and fetch the horses I bartered from the McGuires. I want to take Mary along to help."

My chair tittered on two legs when I jerked backward from the shock. Momma agreed, and the wideness of my smile made my cheeks hurt until I remembered the horses were for the move to Kentucky, which diminished the point of being seen by handsome men. Nonetheless, I had spent a restless night and a fretful morning deciding between my only two outfits.

I signed and turned toward Momma.

"You look so grown-up." She smiled, but her head shook. "Papa may regret taking his young daughter to a fort full of men."

My cheeks flushed. One minute I felt grown, the next childish. But I beamed. *She said I look grown-up.*

"Well, then." Momma rolled and twisted my waist-length braid and sighed as she pinned it up. "Papa is loading the furs on Little Sis. He's ready to get started. Do you have your leggings in your pack for the trip home? It's been a while since you've ridden long-distance."

"Yes, ma'am." I slipped on moccasins, secured my bonnet, and stepped into Momma's hug.

My siblings scurried about preparing for the day and breakfast but paused to kiss my cheeks. George still seemed sullen because Papa told him I could handle horses better and that he was needed here helping Momma manage Gideon behind the plow. I almost felt sorry for him.

Momma draped the strap of my pack over my head and handed me a linen bag of warm hoecakes for Papa's and my breakfast on the road, then kissed my forehead. "Stay close to Papa."

"Yes, ma'am." *Does she think I'll wander off and get lost?*

I smiled and met Papa in the yard, lighting his pipe beside Little Sis. The poor mare hung her head as if humiliated by being treated like a mule. Drummer trotted beside me until Momma called him back to the porch.

Papa squinted at me, then widened his eyes at Momma. "Is this my daughter?"

Momma laughed and stepped inside. His down-turned mouth rose into a half smile. "Well, little miss, are you ready for a long walk to the New River?" He pulled the mare's lead rope and stepped toward the trail.

"Yes, sir." I glanced at the red oak tree bearing Papa's initials as we left the yard and trod along the narrow wagon road.

A woodpecker drummed on a hollow tree nearby. Various chirps, tweets, and cackles from birds made the walk a bit noisy. Occasional daylight shimmered through the leaves and flickered from dew-covered grasses and shrubs that lined our way. I imagined that mischievous fairies enchanted the dew for unsuspecting gnomes to collect for their tea. Once drunk, they would go about doing good deeds instead of bad. I chuckled, then caught up to Papa's brisk pace.

In a few minutes, Papa gazed at me. "What kind of man would make a good husband?"

Heat swept through me as I stopped mid-stride.

He stood still and grinned. "I know you want him handsome like me. But how do you want him to act?"

I stared at my moccasins. "I...I don't know." *I never thought beyond handsome.*

"Men will flock to you like vultures because you are young and pretty. Some will be honorable and worthy, but some will be shiftless or surly. A black bear might look cuddly, and a fox sleek, but both are dangerous."

Surprised by his concern, I chuckled. "I just want to know if I'm pretty."

He grinned and nodded. "Why do you think we're having this conversation? But if men approach to chat with you today, direct them to speak to me. That should curtail the scoundrels. Understand?"

"Yes sir." But I didn't.

He burst into a spirited Irish song about a man marrying one-eyed Reilly's daughter and danced a jig, slapping his leg now and then. I laughed and joined in at the chorus as we resumed our trip. Forest creatures fled before us.

The narrow, lush trail gave way to spacious grassy bottomland as we neared the crossing. I sneezed a couple of times as we waded through the grass.

"I hear this is how Kentucky looks." Papa beamed and spread his arms wide. "My scout friends report that Indian corn grows like weeds in the soil, and game is plentiful and plump."

I didn't flinch. "But corn grows well here, and I like trees and mountains."

He faced me and frowned.

"How many horses are we getting?" I hoped my smile would restore his.

He shook his head and sighed. "Five. In exchange for fifty acres surveyed. I hope Corn's son remembers to meet me at the ford by ten of the clock. If not, I know where they live."

Curiosity peaked. "How old is Mr. McGuire's son?"

Papa laughed. "Has to be at least twenty-one to acquire land." He took a couple of steps before pausing with wide eyes. "Why?"

Orneriness sparked my grin. "Well, maybe I'll run off with him."

He frowned and shook his head but laughed. "I just might have to take a switch to you."

Returning to a serious mood, I asked, "Will you introduce me to him today?"

"Not likely." Papa turned away and quickened the pace down the hill.

Wish I hadn't teased. Maybe he'll change his mind.

As we neared the river, I glanced north and south, but no one approached. Papa didn't seem concerned as he came to a halt beside a brushy area. "Wait out here. I need to relieve myself."

I gasped at the sight of a weeping willow in the center. *The willow tree on his survey?* I pulled my leggings from the saddlebag.

When Papa came out, I went in, parting the sweet-scented honeysuckle vines away from the tree. As I glanced around, I found initials: *WM.* Then I discovered a hollow and peered inside, hoping nothing slept there. But it was too dark to see anything. I poked in a stick, wiggled it about, and waited. Nothing growled or came out. I took a deep breath, plunged my arm inside, and felt around with my hand. The ample space could have easily held documents, but it was bare. I secured my leggings and left the shrubs.

Papa had topped the bank and stood waving to a gray-haired man who led five quarter horses on ropes: three sorrels, a yellow dun, and a dapple gray. My heart sank. *Mr. McGuire's son is elderly. Why didn't Papa just say so?*

Papa examined the sturdy-looking horses, shook hands with the man, and took the ropes. Mr. McGuire tipped his hat in my direction and rode away.

My face flushed as I joined Papa on the bank of the river. "Why didn't you tell me Mr. McGuire's son was aged?"

Papa held his belly, laughing hard and shaking his head. "The son had to leave on a scouting trip yesterday. That was his papa."

Somewhat relieved, I smiled and looked over the horses, partial to the dapple gray.

But Papa began transferring the load of furs to him. "You're going to ride Little Sis until I make sure these geldings are tame enough. Corn McGuire guarantees his son's training, but I have to trust them first. We'll get saddles at the fort. Now, I'll see how this dun responds."

Papa grabbed a handful of black mane, hoisted his leg over its golden back, then spoke in soothing tones as he rubbed the gelding's neck. With a slight nudge, the horse stepped forward, remaining relaxed under Papa's calm manner.

Little Sis nickered and eased into a smooth gait beside the new horses, and Papa and I kept them corralled between us.

I was impressed with how well they obeyed but lamented at not having met their trainer. I also regretted not riding Little Sis more often, for by the time we descended a grassy hill to the fort gate, my inner thighs felt itchy and inflamed in spite of wearing leggings to prevent such. But excitement outweighed misery as I spied tall pickets.

A strong stench of sewage outside the gate triggered gagging. I held my nose, but it didn't help.

Papa chuckled. "Good thing we relieved ourselves in the fresh air of the woods."

The longed-for dream of a thriving, bustling community of families ended as we entered an enclosure of disheveled men dressed in common hunting shirts instead of uniforms. *There'll be no socials in this place.*

Papa led the way to a blockhouse, where we dismounted and secured the horses to a post.

"Stay with the horses," he said. "I'll make the trade, and then we'll get supplies."

He went inside, and I grew nervous. A group of men stopped cleaning their guns to stare at me. I didn't want to be seen anymore, but it was too late. They jutted their chins, tipped their hats, and smiled. Not wanting to be rude, I smiled but turned my attention to the horses.

"Excuse me, ma'am." A deep voice startled me. "Name's Isaiah Brown."

I took a deep breath and turned around.

He had a handsome face in spite of a two-inch scar on his left cheek. But his tobacco-stained teeth, flecked with remnants of the shredded product, ruined his otherwise cheery smile. He turned his head and spat in the dirt as he waited for my response.

My stomach knotted. "I'm sorry, but I can't speak to you without my papa here."

His dark eyes squinted as he grunted. "Just being friendly. What's your name, little miss?"

His manner unnerved me. I'd already told him I couldn't speak with him. I narrowed my eyes and made sure his friends heard. "Leave—me—alone."

He stepped back and spat a plug of tobacco on my moccasin before returning to the other men who jeered at him.

I slung the disgusting wad from my foot and stroked the neck of Little Sis for comfort. *I shouldn't have smiled at them.*

Papa called me from the doorway. "Help me with the supplies."

We toted five saddles, then did all the saddling with not one grown man offering to help.

I lowered the last stirrup and glanced at Papa. "Why are these men so crass?"

"Rough men here, for sure." Papa gave the saddle one last tug. "They're mostly Indian fighters and rogues. Too wild to be family minded. As soon as we load supplies, we'll leave."

The muscles in my arms burned and quivered as I helped Papa heave bags of salt, milled corn, and flour on the dark-red sorrel. Sweat dribbled down my temples by the time boxes of lead ingots, gunpowder, extra rifles, and an assortment of blades were secured between the dapple-gray and light-red geldings. I sat on the ground to catch my breath as Papa draped a heavy tent canvas over of the saddle of the copper-coated horse, along with a large supply of salted pork.

"I need to talk to that man over there." Papa tilted his head in the direction of a man loading survey equipment on a black horse.

I ignored the renewal of hat-tipping from strolling men and watched Papa pull a bundle of papers from inside his hunting shirt. With a quick pace, he made a beeline to the man, handed him the documents in passing, then meandered back as if not in a hurry at all.

What was that about? Guess he changed his mind about talking to him. "Was that a survey?"

"Naw." Papa checked the saddles and gear one more time. "Ready to head home?"

His short answer sent my mind whirling. *What is he up to?*

Sudden whooping from the gate made me jump, and the horses shifted their feet.

A man galloped in with a swirl of dirt. He dismounted, then jumped on a stump in the middle of the yard, waving his hat and shouting. "We're at war." He didn't wait for the gathering crowd. "The British Regulars shot men at

Lexington and Concord three days ago for protecting the powder supply, and the next day, our blame Governor Dunmore removed powder stores from Williamsburg."

Hisses erupted all around us.

Papa pulled my hand. "Follow me." His body shielded me as we tugged the horses toward the gate.

The crowd quieted, and the man resumed. "We can stay in this cesspool or render aid to the provincials of Boston." He raised his sword in the air and yelled, "I stand with Mr. Henry—'Give me liberty or give me death.'"

The men shouted hurrahs and fired weapons into the air.

A surge of excitement shot up my back as fear gripped my stomach.

Our horses startled but didn't bolt. Papa pointed to Little Sis. "Mount up and let's get out of here."

Whoops and gunfire ricocheted from the ridges around us. Fear knotted my gut. We cantered all the way to the river crossing before dismounting to stretch and let the horses graze.

"I'm sorry you had to hear all that." Papa sounded somber. "I'm afraid this is just the beginning. I had hoped to have us in Kentucky territory before this evil started. I'm impressed with our horses, though. Seems that William McGuire did a fine job training. We'll work with them some more, though."

I didn't want to talk about the horses. "How can you remain loyal to a tyrant who sends his troops to kill and oppress his own subjects?"

Papa stumbled back. He might have fallen if not for grabbing his saddle. He took a deep breath and met my stare with a sternness that sent prickles up my back.

"I forbid you from questioning me on this subject again. Remain loyal to me and trust my judgment." He mounted and waded across the river without waiting on me.

I squinted and followed out of duty. *Not allowed to question him. He's never cut me off that way before. Isn't that what King George has done to his subjects?*

When we passed Mr. Thorndike's place, Papa slowed to a walk, then dismounted and waited for me but remained serious. "Which horse do you want?"

His coolness pricked my stony heart. I wanted my papa back. "The dapple gray." My voice quavered. "Please, don't stay angry. I'm sorry."

He reached around me in a hug. "I'm sorry too. Who said you could grow up?"

With a final squeeze to his ribs, I stepped back, drying my face.

He went to work transferring the dapple gray's load to Little Sis, and I walked around to greet the horse, holding out my hand. He bobbed his head at first, then calmed and nudged my arm as if to say, "Let's play." I rubbed his neck, chuckling as his name came to mind. "I'm calling him Patriot."

Papa flinched, then smiled. "Just don't get attached. I had a good horse shot out from under me during the war against the French and Indians."

With a smirk, I mounted Patriot and raised an imaginary sword behind Papa's back. *Give me liberty.*

As Papa and I rode into the yard, Drummer yapped and twirled. Momma stepped on the porch, wiping her hands on her apron, followed by my sisters and Charlie.

George bounced out the door, exclaiming, "Five new horses. Do I get my own?"

Papa dismounted. "Yes. But you need supervision and additional training."

George nodded. "Yes, sir."

Momma smiled as she reached for me. "Did you meet any suitable young men?"

"No, ma'am. Not one." I embraced her and stepped back. "It was a horrible place. They were all rude. Papa said they are mostly Indian fighters."

"That's what I was afraid of. Fort Culbertson was built as a military post about the time Papa returned from the Point."

"Can we pick the horse we want?" Lizzy asked.

I scratched my chosen dapple gray under the neck. "This one's mine. His name's Patriot."

George grinned at me on his way to help Papa unload the yellow dun. "I want to ride this one and name him General."

"You may all choose," Papa said. "But I want to supervise your riding to make sure the horse and rider are a good match."

Momma examined the darkest red sorrel. "This one suits me, but I need to finish supper. Let's get everything unloaded."

We led the horses into the barn, and Papa directed where and how to store the supplies for the trip.

Momma took the littles back to the cabin while the rest of us groomed the horses.

Lizzy conversed with the light red and stroked his neck. "I want to call him Big Red."

"Good," Katie said. "Because I like this fellow." She went to the copper-colored horse. "He has the prettiest eyes and rusty coat. Yes, I'll call him Rusty."

I glanced into the hayloft as Papa's rake scraped the boards. He came to the edge with an armful of fresh hay. "Look out below." A pile landed in the feed trough for the horses.

I covered my mouth and nose with the crook of my arm, waiting for the dust to settle as Papa came down and stretched. "Good day's work. Let's go eat supper."

"I'll be another minute," I said. "Going to the privy first."

When they left, I grabbed the milking stool and climbed the ladder. After wiggling the stool for a sturdy position, I stepped up, looking to the beam, then gasped. The box wasn't there. As I hopped down, I glimpsed it in the corner, partially buried under a pile of older straw used for fodder. I held my breath, scooted to it, and flung open the lid.

An unsealed letter lay on top, which I unfolded with a pounding heart. It was dated 22 March 1775, three days before Papa returned from the McGuire survey a month ago.

I read:

Colonel William Preston to MS

I commend you, sir, for your loyal service to our Royal Governor, Lord Dunmore, and to me in matters regarding surveys in the colony of Virginia. Secrecy is of the utmost importance in light of present political upheaval and for the safety of your family. I appeal to you for steadfast faithfulness in these matters. Firstly, and until further notice, conduct surveys according to British Law in spite of the rulings of the Virginia Convention recently held in Richmond and dispatched into your hand at Wood's. Secondly, maintain friendly terms with all who would oppose the loyalist stance. Be especially mindful of the McGuires, who are associated with men of renown in the patriot circles, until a later course can be determined. Pass information through my courier at Fort Culbertson on the 22nd day of April. lie low a few days, then relay to Fort Cook.

Papa is a traitor! Reeling from shock, I reread, hoping my conclusions were wrong. But clearly, Lord Dunmore and Colonel Preston were loyalists, like Papa, and his association with them placed our family in danger. I witnessed his betrayal of our patriot neighbors today, when he passed documents to the man with the black horse.

Nausea swirled in my belly as I returned the letter and covered the box with straw. Fighting tears, I descended the ladder, dropped the stool beside Helga, and dashed to the privy. I slammed the door behind me, weeping in a rage. *I'm ashamed of you, Papa. How can I act as if nothing is wrong?*

Chapter Six

I poured gooey pancake batter on the cast-iron griddle and stared at Momma as she nursed Sally. The desperation to confide in her crushed my chest. But what if telling her the truth caused trouble between her and Papa? *Would it make a difference? What if she already knows and approves?* I rescued the pancake before it burned, then poured the rest of the batter.

Papa had lied to her. Said he had to go to Cook's Fort this afternoon so he could sign on with the road crew in the morning. But I knew about his orders from Colonel Preston. The same information he passed into the loyalist's hands at Culberson's twelve days ago he would deliver to loyalists at Cook's by nightfall.

Papa sat the bucket of warm frothy milk on the floor when he entered. "I've raked out a corner of the barn for straw beds. Need help after breakfast, making it comfortable for the men before I fetch them from

Thorndike. We'll stop at the field on the way in, and I'll show them what to do while I'm gone."

Feigning surveying while the slaves do your work. I glared.

"I'll have the men here in time for lunch. Do you object to them eating with us?"

Sally toddled away as Momma stood. "No, makes it easier." She strained the milk through a cheesecloth. "Let's eat."

After breakfast, Momma followed Katie, George, and me into the yard. She went to the chicken pen while we carried all the extra quilts to the barn. As we laid the quilts on a barrel, a hen squawked outside and then fell silent with a chop on the butchering stump.

Katie and I gasped at each other.

"Why did Momma do that?" she asked.

I had no explanation. Sacrificing a good layer was usually an honor reserved for important company.

"Yay, stewed chicken." George beamed and went straight to work, scooping up armfuls of fresh hay as Papa heaved it from the loft.

I sneezed and shook my head before turning to the task. *Nothing makes sense anymore.*

Katie and I helped toss hay into two piles in the front corner, where a hemp rope stretched between two posts. We draped wool blankets over the ropes to make the partition and spread the quilts over the piles.

I brushed my hand over the nine-patch quilt to smooth it and tucked it all around the straw to make a pallet. The straw pallets looked comfortable, and the partition softened the barn's appearance. The small, shuttered window allowed fresh air, but it was still a barn, complete with chickens running about, squabbling over crickets and beetles.

George leapt from behind me and pounced in the middle of a pallet, before rolling off laughing. He tried to make his escape, but Katie stuck her foot out. He landed on his stomach with a smack and a moan.

I grabbed his arm and helped him up. "You will remake the bed."

He dusted off and shot a venomous glare at Katie. "I just wanted to test it."

Papa chuckled from the loft, then came down the ladder carrying his box.

I gulped. *Does he know I snooped?*

He set it on the ground, opened it in front of us, and carried the documents to his saddlebags flanking Little Sis. In a moment, he spun on the heel of his boot and faced us. "Take your horses out together and train them to stand still when we shoot. They were a little skittish at Fort Culbertson. Dismount first, though. Allow them a foot length of rope in case they move and use a gentle tug to retrieve. Go ahead and check the traps while you're out." He picked up the box and placed it in my hands, smiling. "Put this in the tobacco shed for me, please."

My heart raced as I nodded. If he knew about my nosiness, this was a merciful way to break me.

"Be safe out there and don't kill each other." He smirked and mounted Little Sis, then led Momma's and Lizzy's horses behind him for the slaves to ride back.

George sneered at me on his way to saddle General. I looked back to make sure he finished smoothing the hay bed.

Katie had already saddled Rusty and stood in front of him with a handful of oats.

"I'll be back in a bit." With the box on my hip, I shooed the hens from the barn and closed the door behind me to keep them out.

I approached the tall rectangular shed with caution, watching for wasps' nests near the door or just inside. The door creaked a bit as I eased it open. An earth-scented breeze circulated with the sweet smell of crushed beechnuts as I placed the box on the plank floor, then sat on it. The day seemed full of trouble already, and I didn't know how to sort out my jumbled thoughts. Momma said God helps resolve problems if we ask him, but problems were heaping up quicker than his solutions. *What is Papa up to now? Dare I talk to him again?* I hoped to hear God's gentle whisper in my ear, but a mosquito buzzed it instead. *Never mind.* I concluded my prayer and rubbed the itch on my cheek.

Katie was in a huff, as usual, when I entered the yard. "It's about time. What took you so long? Let's go." She slid the rifle into the scabbard on the saddle and mounted Rusty. George hopped into his saddle on General and followed Katie into a quick gait.

"Wait for me." I tugged on the saddle girth to make sure it was tight, then mounted and clicked my tongue for Patriot to gallop.

They seemed quite pleased with themselves for leaving me.

"Do you want me to tell Papa the two of you rushed into the woodlands without caution? There could still be Shawnee scouts about, you know. Or have you forgotten their old trail is nearby?"

I dismounted and walked along, checking for signs to make my point, satisfied by the sufficient fear registering on their faces as they dismounted.

George stepped in front of me. "Papa and I haven't found any signs. And he said they wouldn't come back this way. There could be bear, though. Sorry for leaving you." He pointed to a crop of bushes. "The first trap is over here. Can I shoot first?"

"No," Katie said. "You and Mary get more practice firing than I do. I'll go first." She glared, as if waiting for us to argue.

"I was going to suggest it, anyway." I wiggled my head. "George is stronger than you and can help me hold the horses. Wait for us to remove their bits first, in case they jerk."

She sighed and retrieved the gun.

George and I held the horses' ropes loose while Katie stepped forward and loaded.

She knelt on one knee and propped her elbow on the other, steadying the barrel before aiming. "That sycamore tree over there."

The blast rang in my ears as the limbs on the tree trembled from the impact of the shot. Rusty jerked his head but didn't bolt. General flared his nostrils, and Patriot pulled his ears back with a slight twitch.

George dropped the reins and rushed to look at the tree. He glanced back, beaming. "Hurrah. She hit it dead center. Good shooting, Katie." He dug the lead shot from the tree with his hunting knife, then dropped it into his pouch. "I hear a rabbit squealing in the trap. Want me to fetch it?"

I nodded and stroked Patriot's neck. "Good boy. Mr. McGuire trained you well." I whispered in his ear. "I wish you could tell me about him."

Katie handed me the gun, beaming. "How did Rusty do?"

"He needs a little practice. Not bad, but he jerked."

She rubbed Rusty's neck. "We'll see how he does on the next shot. Maybe he'll do better with me holding him."

George hung the rabbit upside down on a broken branch to bleed.

I took the rifle to him. "Your turn to shoot."

"Naw, you go ahead. I can't beat Katie's shot, but I want to see you do it."

Somewhat confident, I loaded the barrel, primed, and cocked. "Ready?"

"Yes," they said together.

I aimed, held my breath, then lowered the gun. My ears rang as if I'd fired. My heartbeat raced. *I almost shot Papa.*

"What's wrong with you?" Katie asked.

George stared at me.

Confused and embarrassed, I handed the rifle to George. "I don't feel well." I stepped away and hid behind a cluster of shrubs, stifling sobs. The image of Papa's bleeding head unnerved me, as if I had just shot him. I didn't understand.

A shot rang out, and George bragged, "Just below your shot."

"Rusty twitched a little but stayed still," Katie said. "Let's get to the other traps and go home. It's hot already. If you're ill, George and I can check the rest of the traps so you can go home."

Leaving them behind to escape my shame wasn't an option. "I'm all right now." I dried my face and came out of seclusion. After mounting Patriot, I glanced at George. "Lead us to the next trap."

When we neared the top of the ridge, the horses stopped without warning, snorted, and raised their heads. I turned to at Katie. "Reload. Something's spooking them."

My heart raced as Katie whipped the gun from the scabbard and balanced it across her lap and the saddle. I scanned the area, knowing Katie would have to make the shot if needed. *She won't freeze.* Katie bit the top off a paper cartridge and poured the contents into the barrel. She stuffed the paper in for wadding, then slid the ramrod from the holder, but the rifle fell to the ground.

I gasped, dismounted, and retrieved the weapon as the leaves rustled. Katie tossed me the rod. Propping the butt against a tree, I tamped the barrel. "Ease the horses back down. I'll keep watch."

The horses snorted as they turned, and Katie and George headed away with Patriot.

A low growl preceded a squalling cougar's leap onto a rock ledge in front of me with bared fangs and yellow eyes. I aimed for his chest and fired. The cat flipped in the air and landed on the ground, dead.

Did I do that? My legs wobbled as I sat on the ground with my heart racing.

George shouted, "Whew, you got him. I'll drape him over my saddle to take home. Nice fur."

Katie sniffled as she knelt beside me and wrapped her arms around my shoulders. "Oh, Mary, what if I hadn't dropped the gun? I would have been too scared to fire."

I couldn't hold back sobs. She rocked me, and I let her. *What if I'd allowed them to go to the ridge without me? What if I'd lost my nerve again or missed?* Somehow, I'd acted quickly and without fear.

George interrupted. "We need to get to the last trap. There's nothing left at this one. Reckon that's why the cougar threatened. We interrupted his breakfast. At least the last trap is close to the cabin."

Katie stood and helped me to my feet, but I was still shaky. She and George held my arms and walked me to Patriot. They had to hoist me into the saddle.

George reloaded, slid the barrel into the scabbard, and mounted. He sat tall in the saddle and cleared his throat. "I don't think we should tell Momma about the cougar."

I nodded and followed him.

"I agree," Katie said. "Momma has enough to worry over with slaves coming and Papa leaving again. Why can't he wait until he takes the slaves back to sign on with the road crew?"

"You know what I think?" George slowed to a stop and peered at us. "I think Papa is doing some Indian scouting along with surveying. I sneaked a look at one of his surveys the other day and read a note that said, 'Report Wood's findings upon arrival at Fort Cook.' Papa caught me before I could put it back in that box he took down from the loft."

I shook my head but didn't refute his claim. *So that's why Papa's not using the box.*

Katie glared at me. "You've looked at his surveys, too."

George's jaw dropped. "You have?"

I swallowed. *How much do I say?* "I have. And he might be scouting, but I would wager Momma doesn't know. But what did Papa do to you?"

George took a deep breath. "He scolded me fierce and made me promise to stay out of his things. He said there are men counting on his sacred honor in matters that don't concern me."

"But he said the Indians won't raid again." Katie shifted in her saddle and frowned. "Why scout unless there's trouble?"

George stroked his chin. "Well, I heard him tell Momma the Shawnee would remain loyal to the Crown, but those for liberty are trying to make them allies so they won't raid."

My breath caught. "Enough talk. My head is about to burst." I gave Patriot rein and galloped to the last trap, screaming curses under my breath. I ripped a handful of pine needles from an overhead bough, dropped all but a few, and bit down. The tangy juice numbed my tongue and eased my headache by the time we stopped. I looked into the clear sky. *God, please, no. I can't deal with Indian raids again.*

George dismounted and dispatched a rabbit in the trap while Katie and I waited. The desire to talk to Papa about the Indians weighed heavily, but I couldn't give up George. I sighed.

As we neared the yard, Drummer pranced toward me. I dismounted into a squat, patting my leg for the spaniel to come. When I sat cross-legged, he rolled onto his back in my lap. I smiled and rubbed his belly, purposely delaying the meeting of slaves and having to be pleasant to Papa.

I called to George and Katie as they continued toward the barn. "Take care of the horses, and I'll clean the game."

George pointed toward the tobacco field. "The slaves are here."

I cringed and stood. Papa and two dark-skinned men were walking about. One appeared tall and the other shorter, but stout. I mounted and rushed to catch up with Katie and George.

Chapter Seven

Katie and I carried the meat into the cabin and laid it on the chopping board.

"We got a couple of rabbits," I said.

Momma wiped her forehead on her sleeve. "Good. I didn't know how to make this hen stretch enough for two more at our table. Hand me a couple of those bay leaves, then chop a handful of onion grass to throw into the pot."

I sighed, and Momma noticed.

"No more of that."

"Yes, ma'am. I'm sorry. But I don't like Papa bringing slaves." The words sounded arrogant as they escaped, but I couldn't explain them.

Her silence was agonizing. A lump rose in my throat as she wiped her hands on her apron and turned to me with a solemn expression. "We have an opportunity to show these men kindness while they are in our care. Papa has my blessing to supply them with extra provisions for their work. We will treat them with all the dignity and respect we would any stranger to our home. Is that understood?" She raised her eyebrows, glanced around the dim cabin at my siblings, and then back to me.

"Yes, ma'ams" echoed.

In spite of the scolding, I smiled. Momma's opinion of the matter filled me with peace.

Loud thumps preceded the door flinging open to Papa and George as they rolled two stumps to the table. A couple of silhouettes hesitated in the doorway.

Momma waved them inside. "Welcome to our table."

They looked wide-eyed and shook their heads, but Momma smiled and pointed to the stumps.

Papa nodded. "It's okay. Please sit."

They stared at the floor and entered. Their dingy linen shirts were tattered, and they reeked of body odor and turpentine. Hard-soled shoes bore holes on the sides, exposing their stockings.

"Thank you," the larger of the two men whispered in a deep voice.

Papa introduced them. "This gentleman is Big Jim, and this is Adam."

"Pleased to meet you," Momma said.

I didn't know what to say; the whole thing was awkward. Big Jim looked scary. He was massive, with bulging muscles and hands that looked as if he could squeeze the life out of me with one grip. He didn't look directly at me, but his smile was timid. I looked away, realizing I had made him uncomfortable with my stares.

I knew that some slaves came from a faraway land called Africa, but Big Jim's speech had sounded English. "Where were you born?"

Big Jim seemed shocked by my directness. He looked at Papa.

Papa smiled and nodded.

Big Jim gazed at the floor, then at me. "We was born on Masta Thorndike's place. But my momma was born near Williamsburg, same as Adam's."

Adam glanced up, smiling. "Masta Thorndike bring our mommas up this way when they was young. Our mommas have the same grandparents—bringed to Virginia from Senegal land." He lowered his eyes.

Big Jim grinned and nodded. "Adam be my cousin."

I wanted to ask more questions, but Momma put her finger to her lips to hush me. I hadn't meant to be rude. They seemed like normal folks.

Charlie rubbed Adam's arm with his hand as if trying to wipe something off. "Muddy."

Adam smiled but didn't have a chance to answer before Momma intervened. "Hush and let them eat."

After a few bites of bacon, I glanced at the men who sat with folded hands. Empty plates lay before them, swiped clean of every morsel, including gravy.

"We have plenty. Would you like more?" Papa asked.

Their heads shook at the same time, then Adam spoke. "No, sir. We be full. Jest used to eatin' quick like."

Papa scraped up his last crumb and sat back. "I've shown the men where to start, and they know where their quarters are for the night. I'll be back by noon tomorrow. If you men are ready, I'll walk you out."

"Yes, sir." Big Jim stood, bowing his head toward Momma. "Thank you for the fine vittles, missus."

"Yes'm. Thank you." Adam rose and followed Big Jim and Papa outside.

They seemed pleasant and likable, but Big Jim's eyes were lifeless, and I wondered why.

After Papa prepared Little Sis, said his goodbyes, and rode up the northeast trail, the men went straight to the field.

Momma secured her bonnet, then handed a small basket each to Sally and Charlie before taking their free hands. She glanced at George. "Carry one of the rifles and follow me to the tobacco field. We'll gather grubs for the chickens while Big Jim and Adam turn up the ground. The rest of you take hoes to the garden and do the same. Mary and Katie will thin the corn seedlings."

I waited until Momma was out of hearing before I released an irritated sigh. Making Big Jim and Adam do all that work so we could plant tobacco for someone else's profit still didn't make sense. The sudden realization that Big Jim and Adam worked for others all the time with no benefits whatsoever made my cheeks flush. *Who am I to complain?* I shook my head and met my sisters, leaving the barn with baskets.

Katie smiled and tilted her head toward the barn door. "We piled the hoes in the wheelbarrow for you to bring."

Sweltering air made pushing the creaking wheelbarrow along the rocky path burdensome. When I stopped to wipe sweat from my brow, huge fluffy clouds were blowing west but they weren't drooping, which meant it would rain by late afternoon, somewhere else. I gasped. *Kentucky lies west, and we'll be traversing mountains through August and September. Will tent canvas be enough protection from storms?*

"Hey," Katie yelled. "Are you going to get over here with that cart sometime today? It's too hot out here to be wasting time."

"Sorry, I'm coming." I jerked the cart forward, remembering the Bible verse "Today has enough trouble," but miseries filled my mind just the same. There would be two months' worth of weather, bugs, snakes, and nighttime varmints sniffing out our food.

At the garden, Susie and Nancy followed behind Lizzy, dropping grubs into their baskets as she hoed. Katie and I went to our own rows, two feet apart.

In a few minutes, Katie peered at me with a frown. "Do you think Momma is worried about the slaves?"

I scooted down my row, moving my gun along the ground, within arm's reach, and slowly snipped off the weakest seedlings with my fingernail as I answered, "I don't think so. Why?"

"She seemed troubled to me. Like she didn't like Papa leaving us alone with them. You don't think they would try to harm us, do you?"

I paused to look at her. "Of course not. Now hush. No sense in thinking that way. They seem respectful enough. And Momma would shoot them herself if she felt threatened. Maybe she's just burdened by how much there is to do before the move to Kentucky in three months. I don't think she is as strong as we think."

"Well, I need her to be, or I would crumble like this dirt clod and blow away." Katie tossed a handful of dirt into the hot breeze.

As dirt blew toward me, I turned my head and closed my eyes, then glared at her, shaking dirt from my bonnet. "Stop being so dramatic and get back to work."

"I didn't mean to get dirt in your face, but you don't have to be so mean." She pooched her lips. "I'm going to the creek to cool off."

"Take the bucket and bring back fresh water."

She grabbed the bucket but ignored me and marched toward the creek.

"I want to go." Nancy dropped her basket on the ground and stood, waiting.

Susie shook dirt from her petticoat. "And me."

Katie shook her head. "No. Stay with Mary. I want to be alone."

I shrugged my shoulders at the girls. "Katie's just mad. Finish your row, and we'll take a break."

"Well, if she thinks I'm going to finish her row, she's mistaken." Lizzy huffed. Then she looked into the sky. "Do you think it's going to rain? I hate being caught in the rain."

"Me too. But the clouds are headed west." I resumed hoeing.

A moment later, Katie's screams erupted from the creek. I grabbed the rifle and shouted, "Stay here." My sisters huddled with fearful faces.

Drummer and I raced down the wooded path toward the creek, but stopped a few feet back. A swarm of yellow jackets hovered above the water near the bank. Katie swam away, immersed. I ran in the direction she was headed. She popped her head up, bawling as she waded out of the water and collapsed on the bank. Her lips and neck were swelling. I ran into woods for a remedy and found a clump of egg-shaped plantain leaves. I crushed them in my hand so they would be sticky and returned to Katie's side. "Stop crying so you can breathe."

She calmed to a sniffle and drew shallow breaths while I wrapped her neck with the leaves to draw out the venom.

I removed my apron, doused it in the creek, and gave it to Katie. "Hold this on your lips to keep down the swelling."

Katie applied the cloth and whimpered as I helped her stand. "Can you walk?"

She nodded.

I waved to Lizzy as we emerged from the woods and yelled, "Bring the wheelbarrow."

"What happened?" She grabbed the handles and ran toward us.

"Yellow jackets. I have to get Katie to the cabin. Tell Susie and Nancy to bring home the hoes, then hurry to the barn and ride Big Red out to the field and fetch Momma."

As Lizzy sprinted away, Katie plopped into the wheelbarrow in a heap, which caused it to topple and her to fall on her elbow. She stood, shaking her head, mumbling what sounded like "I'd rather walk."

"I'll follow behind, pushing it in case you need to rest before reaching home."

She nodded and staggered forward.

Drummer trotted along until we reached the yard, then he went to the spring. Katie was a little out of breath by the time we made it to the cabin. Lizzy ran past us into the barn.

After helping Katie to Momma's bed, I scooped a handful of Papa's dried tobacco into my palm and spat on it to make a paste. I put a linen towel under Katie's head, removed the plantain leaves, and patted the tobacco paste around her neck up to her lips to finish drawing the poison out of the stings. Katie relaxed. I took the container of honey and dipped out a spoonful for her to swallow. *Momma always says it helps ease itching.*

Katie squeezed my hand and mouthed, "Thank you."

I stroked her head and smiled. "Momma will be here soon."

Susie and Nancy entered the cabin a couple of minutes later, wide-eyed. Susie whispered. "Is she going to die?" Tears streamed down Nancy's cheeks.

I put my arms around them. "No, she hurts, and the venom is making her sleepy. Momma will be here soon."

Momma stomped onto the porch, then rushed in, throwing her bonnet on the table. She wiped her sweaty brow and blew out a deep breath.

"Katie's breathing is good," I assured her.

Momma examined Katie and smiled. "Good job. The swelling has already gone down. I counted at least sixteen stings." She took my hands. "I'm proud of your sober-minded thinking."

"Thank you, Momma." My eyes teared.

Relief swept over me as Katie sat up, holding on to the towel. Her swollen lips made her speech muffled as she told us what happened, but all of her words started with a T.

I had to concentrate to understand.

She wiped her eyes, shrugged, and concluded, "Toun't toe tere tha tucket tent."

Susie giggled. "What did she say?"

"She saw the nest too late and had to roll into the creek and swim away." I translated. "She thought she was going to drown. And she doesn't know where the bucket went."

Katie nodded, and her lips parted in a slight smile.

Momma laughed and wet a clean towel for Katie's lips. "We'll have to find the nest so we don't stumble upon it again. Stay in bed and rest awhile longer. I need to check on supper." She turned to me. "There's no need to supervise Big Jim and Adam. They have almost an acre of hills mounded. I told them to work another hour, then come in to rest before supper."

My mouth fell opened. *That's nearly 250 hills.*

"Lizzy is walking Charlie and Sally to the garden, along with George. Secure Big Red in the barn for me and take Susie and Nancy out to help them finish up there. You can bring Charlie and Sally back here for naps and tend to the barn chores for George."

"Might we ride Big Red to the garden?" I asked.

"No." Momma turned toward me. "He reared up with Lizzy and tried to come back to the barn. He's too much horse for her, and he's getting away with being wild. I don't want any of you on him until Papa can settle him down."

"Yes, ma'am." *Why hasn't Lizzy mentioned his behavior?* "May I ride Patriot? He's gentle. It will be faster to get the babies home."

Momma nodded.

"We have to go back to the garden?" Susie whined. "I can help with supper."

"You are needed in the garden helping Nancy." Momma shot a piercing glance at Susie.

"If you run, I bet you and Nancy will beat me there before you can count to one hundred."

I grinned, but they frowned and went out the door ahead of me.

Big Red jerked his head when I took his rope. I held him firmly and rubbed his neck. "Now, see here." I stared into his eye. "You have to follow me to the barn. It's your own fault you can't go." His intense gaze unnerved me. I gave the rope a gentle tug, and he followed. Drummer crawled out of his hole under the porch, panting. "Stay, boy," I told him.

As I entered the barn, Susie flew passed me counting, with the hoes bouncing in the wheelbarrow and Nancy running to keep up. I laughed and took my time saddling Patriot. As I walked him out, Big Red whinnied from the stall.

After mounting, I peered ahead and waited until my sisters neared the garden gate before easing into a trot.

As I slowed to a halt, Lizzy ran to me, asking, "How's Katie?"

"Sleepy and sore but doing well. I need to take Charlie and Sally home for naps. Why didn't you tell anyone about Big Red's defiance?"

Her face reddened. "It's not his fault. I don't know how to make him mind. Papa will help me with him when he's home."

I nodded, then Lizzy hoisted Sally in front of me and Charlie behind. "Thank you. Sorry you're having to finish for Katie."

"Well, I'm glad she's all right." Lizzy backed away.

Patriot kept a slow, smooth pace back in spite of Sally's wiggly feet tapping his neck and Charlie's constant squirming. When we arrived, Momma retrieved the children from the saddle. I walked Patriot into the barn and dismounted. When Big Red stretched his head toward me, I stepped back and laughed. "What? You think you deserve a neck rub?" I scratched his neck. "Stop being so ornery to my sister, you ol' devil. Papa's going to teach you better."

When I finished in the barn, George pushed the wheelbarrow inside and glanced around. "Thank you for taking care of the barn. I'm tired."

"Me too." I smiled and wiped sweat from my temples with the back of my hand went to the spring to wash. Susie and Nancy dumped the basket of grubs into the chicken pen and ran squealing as the hens feasted. Big Jim and Adam chuckled as they came upon the scene. I met them before they entered the barn. "The horses are groomed and fed, so they should settle down soon. Momma is almost finished with supper."

Big Jim smiled. "Yes'm. Please ask her if we can eat in the barn. We be more comfortable out here, 'cause your papa be away."

"Yes, sir, I'll tell her."

He shook his head. "No, miss. Youse not to call us sir."

"Why not?"

Adam looked at his feet. "It's not proper. We be slaves."

"Well, we have different rules." I smiled and followed my siblings into the cabin.

I relayed Big Jim's request. Momma packed a basket with large helpings of stewed hen and squirrel, along with fresh hoecakes.

She wiped her hands on her apron and handed me the basket. "Knock first, so they aren't caught off guard."

"Yes, ma'am."

As I neared the barn door, Big Jim shouted, "Hush that kinda talk."

I jumped, then stood still and listened.

"But this be our best chance." Adam spoke with venom. "Once the mastas round here gets wind of the governor's pass for all us to flee the rebs, there won't be no way to gets to Williamsburg to join the fight against um. We can be long gone 'fore Mr. Shirley be back. We done hilled up most of the mounds he say to do."

"I sayed no." Big Jim's voice boomed. "Mr. Shirley be a good man. He be blamed if we runs off. Now, I say hush 'fore I smack your mouth."

Adam didn't say anything more.

My stomach churned. *Governor Dunmore told the slaves to run away and join the Regulars.* I waited a long two minutes before knocking. Somehow, I had to pretend I hadn't heard anything. My heart raced as I knocked again.

"Yes'm. Come in," Big Jim said.

I clenched my jaw and entered, clearing the phlegm from my throat. "I brought supper."

"Thank you, little miss." Adam grinned.

His grin annoyed me. I glared, then turned to Big Jim and handed him the basket with a smile.

"Have a good evening." I waited for him to look at me, which he did briefly. "Thank you for helping my papa."

He kept his eyes on his shoes. "Our pleasure, miss. You been kind. Now, we best eat and rest for the morrow."

I couldn't help glaring at Adam again. He studied me as if trying to discern my knowledge of the conversation. I swallowed hard and smiled at him with my best fake smile before leaving the barn. I didn't know if I should tell Momma about the conversation. Big Jim seemed to have squelched Adam's plan to run away while they were under Papa's agreement. But should Mr. Thorndike be informed of Adam's intent? Did Big Jim want to run away too? I didn't want Big Jim to be in trouble. I sighed and decided to keep their secret.

Chapter Eight

Cougars transformed into screaming Shawnee as they chased me through the dark forest. One hit me with a saddlebag, which ended up being Katie's straw stuffed pillow, startling me awake.

"You were moaning and kicking the floor," she said, as if I could have helped it.

I dressed in a foul mood, then descended the ladder into a rambunctious scene of Charlie dancing around a giggling Sally. He sang a made-up song about birds chirping, which I was sure to hum the rest of the day.

"Be still." I scanned the room. "Where's Momma?"

"'Side." Charlie grinned, pointing to the door.

Nancy stood from rolling the pallets to the wall. "She's teaching Susie how to milk Helga."

A moment later, the door opened, and Susie entered with a basket of eggs. Momma followed, lugging in a full bucket of milk. I waited until she set it on the counter, then hugged her, laying my head on her shoulder, wanting her reassurance that all my worries would come out in the wash. "Good morning."

Her head met mine. "Thank you. I needed that. I've been feeling the weight of all there is to do of late."

Surprised by her admission, I stepped back to glimpse a slight smile. She kissed my forehead and moved aside. "Big Jim and Adam must have wanted to get started early. They've already gone," she said.

I gasped. *Surely, they wouldn't run away in broad daylight.*

Momma's head tilted with a frown. "What's wrong?"

"Everything." My eyes watered, wishing I could say.

She put her arms around me. "Yes indeed. There is much to be concerned about. But all we can do is pray and hope everything will come out in the wash." She released me and turned to strain the milk.

Worry remained. *What if they fled? I have to check.* "May I forage? I saw a good patch of dandelions in the meadow near the tobacco field."

She dried her hands on her apron and smiled. "Yes. And please take Charlie for a while. He's big enough to help now."

"Yes, ma'am." I grinned but waited for her to turn her back before sighing. *Not what I had in mind.*

George's quick scuttle down the ladder captured my attention.

"Katie said she can't go with me to check traps on account of her stings." He frowned.

"She seemed well enough when she woke me," I scoffed.

Katie stepped from the ladder, straightened her back, and walked as if balancing a book on her head, which I wanted to knock off.

Momma assessed her face and neck. "The swelling is down, and your breathing is normal. Guarding your brother in the forest is less strenuous than digging roots and plucking leaves."

Katie stared wide-eyed, frowning. "Yes, ma'am."

I took a bite of warm oat groats and smirked at her. *Serves you right.*

George stood, gulping his milk and gathering his hoecakes into a cloth. "Let's go."

"The trapped varmints won't flee before we get there." Katie glared. "I can't eat fast. My lips are sore."

He grabbed the rifle and cartridge box, then placed his breakfast in the knapsack before handing it to Katie. "Wrap them for later. I saw deer tracks yesterday morning. Papa will be proud if we get one. Drummer will sniff it out, and General can carry it back."

She finished her bite with a sigh and strode out the door behind George.

Momma shook her head and gathered the bowls from the table. "Land that boy thinks he's grown."

After helping with dishes, Lizzy and Susie gathered baskets and knives, then raced out the door. Momma sighed and sat with Sally in the rocker.

"Are you ill?" I asked.

She smiled. "Needing a quiet moment to pray about things. Thank you. We'll come directly."

I helped Nancy tie her bonnet under her chin and took Charlie's hand. "Let's go to work."

As we passed the garden fence, Lizzy and Susie were collecting comfrey leaves.

"Remember not to touch your lips or noses," I said. "The sticky hairs will seal them closed, and you won't be able to breathe."

"We know," Lizzy said, and continued picking.

To my relief, Big Jim and Adam were in the tobacco field, hard at work. In the meadow, I squatted in front of a cluster of bright-yellow dandelions. "See these?" I spoke to Charlie and plucked one. "Break them off and put them in the basket."

"Want me to pick these?" Nancy pointed to sage leaves.

I nodded. "Just don't wipe your eyes."

When I glanced back, Charlie had wandered into the woods behind me. He peeked from behind a large oak tree. "Find."

"Stop that and come here. We can play hide-and-seek later."

He slapped his leg with his hat and pooched his lips as he approached. I turned back to pick dandelion leaves but heard the crunching of leaves from his running feet.

I sprang to my feet. "Charlie, get back here."

He disappeared inside thick brush before I reached the tree line. "Come here at once, or I'll take you back to Momma."

I parted bushes and crawled on my knees under vines to watch for his legs. Finally, I stood to listen for leaves rustling or twigs breaking. When I made it to the creek trail, I found his hat. "Come out, Charlie—you win. I can't find you. We have work to do now." As I waited for him to answer, my face grew hot. I yelled. "Where are you?" *How did he get away so fast? He's not yet three.* I stomped down the trail until I saw where he had trampled his way through some tall marshy grass. "Can you hear me?" I asked.

A soft whimper preceded a cracking tree branch, then a splash took my breath. I tore through the brambles toward the creek, praying, *God. No.* Sharp sticks and rocks slashed my feet as I slogged through ankle-deep mud to the bank. *Why did I go back to picking dandelions instead of making him come?*

A rotted tree lay snapped in two over a deep inlet that flowed into the creek, but no Charlie. I maneuvered around thick brush and lifted my petticoat to my knees, wading into the swift current. Several yards ahead, my breath caught at the sight of him trapped inside a tangle of tree roots on the opposite bank.

I cried out, "God, no! Help me," and swished toward Charlie as fast as I could over sharp stones. *This can't be happening.*

He thrashed the water, trying to free himself, but slipped further under. His head bobbed up and down as he fought the current. *Six more yards.*

I screamed, "Hold on. I'm coming."

But as I rushed toward him, my foot slipped on an algae-coated rock, and I landed hard on my rear. Pain shot up my spine. I pushed up to my feet, weeping and peering at Charlie. He wasn't moving anymore. His face lay forward in the water. I yelled, "Charlie, raise your head. Breathe. Please don't be drowned."

"Miss Mary." Someone called my name, but I couldn't answer. "Miss Mary, go come back. I gots him." Adam appeared from the thick brush ahead of me and waded out toward Charlie, then plunged into the water. Adam's arm bled as he lifted the limp body from the tangle. Charlie's head fell against Adam's chest as he was rushed from the creek.

No! He can't be dead. Please, no. The agony in my chest matched the pain in my tailbone with each step toward the bank.

Adam laid Charlie on the ground sideways, patting him hard on the back. "Come on now, little masta. You can't go. You stays down here." Adam spoke as if Charlie could hear.

I knelt beside him, sobbing. "How will I tell Momma I let you get away?"

The next pat produced coughing, sputtering, and then vomiting as Adam sat him up. "There you is. Youse all right now, little masta. Youse gonna live."

Charlie wrapped his arms around Adam's neck, crying.

Adam brought him to me as I cringed to sit. "Your sister be here."

I cuddled and rocked Charlie as we cried in each other's arms for a moment, then I pulled him back to examine him. He had some cuts and a big red knot on his forehead. I felt for broken bones along his arms and legs, but he didn't flinch.

Adam sat behind Charlie and rubbed his back. "Now, I tells you the truth, little masta. There be a bad serpent lurking in creeks, rivers, an' such waitin' to pull children that wanders off down to the pit. Now, mind what I say, 'cause he 'bout had you, and poor ol' Adam had a terrible time a-snatchin' you back."

Charlie peered toward the creek with big eyes and tumbled back into Adam's lap. The man stood with him. "I best help you get him to his momma."

I wanted to hug him, too. "Thank you for being here to save Charlie. Please rush him home. Don't wait on me."

I rolled to my side and onto my feet, holding my breath as I stood.

"Yes'm." Adam's stride quickened.

Searing pain made walking slow. I wiped a tear from my cheek. *How do I face Momma? I let Charlie get away. He almost died, and it's my fault.* I drew a deep breath and watched Adam enter the yard ahead of me. My stomach knotted as he reached the porch calling, "Missus Shirley."

Momma stepped onto the porch with her face twisted in fear. "What happened?"

"He 'bout drown, ma'am. But he come to and throwed up the water."

She glanced at me and motioned for him to follow her inside. I allowed tears to stream down my cheeks. "Bring him to the table," Momma said.

Upon reaching the porch, I held on to a post and heaved myself up, cringing.

Inside, Momma had Charlie stripped down and was raising and bending his arms and legs and pressing on his ribs. She put her ear against his back and listened. "Take a deep breath. Sounds clear." She snuggled him in a blanket, and sat with him in the rocker, looking up at Adam. "Thank you for saving my boy."

I eased in front of Momma, sniffling. "I'm sorry. He sneaked away from me to play, and by the time I got to the creek"—A breath heaved, and sobs erupted again. I wiped my eyes and cleared my throat—"I couldn't reach him." I hunched toward Charlie, brushed his tangled hair from his forehead, and kissed his cheek. "I'm sorry I fussed at you. I love you." He smiled weakly and closed his eyes. I peered at Momma. "Will he be all right?"

She smiled and nodded. I stood and turned to Adam. "Somehow, God sent Adam to pull Charlie out."

Adam shook his head. "No, ma'am. I just be at the creek drawing water when I seen him come my way. I thanks the Lord I knows how to swim though. Little masta was catched in a good-sized branch what saved him. I just untangles and brings him in, like a fish from the net. Well ma'am, I best get back 'fore Big Jim thinks I runned off." He tipped his hat and headed out the door.

"No, sir. You sit down at the table and let Mary dress your wound. It's bleeding." She looked at me. "His gash might need some stitches. Are you up to it? I need to tend to Charlie."

"Yes, ma'am." I wiped my face with my apron and washed my hands.

"Thank you, little miss." Adam sat at the table and stretched his arm out.

Momma laid Charlie on her bed and returned with needle, thread, and strips of linen to use as bandages. "Use this tincture of willow bark to clean everything first."

I soaked a clean linen rag and dabbed it on Adam's wound, fascinated by the way his coal-black skin seemed to shimmer in the light while he squinted his eyes and clenched his jaw.

"Sorry." I sighed and pricked the raw inside layer of his skin with the needle. He sucked in a deep breath with each stick but barely flinched. I focused on drawing his dark skin layers back together in a straight line, then tied a knot and snipped off the end with a clean knife. "There. I hope it holds. I left enough at the end for you to snip off in a few days."

Adam took a deep breath and looked at the stitches. "Looks mighty fine, little miss."

Momma applied willow salve to the wound and wrapped the bandages around it. "Be easy with your arm a few days. Don't let it get wet."

"Yes'm. Thank you." Adam tipped his hat to Momma and went to the door. "I must get back to the field."

Momma nodded, and he stepped out.

I blinked away tears, thanking God for Adam. *What if Papa hadn't needed to borrow them? Charlie would be dead.* A shudder ran down my spine, sending a twinge of pain to my rear. I turned to Momma. "Now, I need a poultice. My foot slipped in the creek, and I landed on a rock."

"Land sakes." Momma shook her head as she walked to the cabinet. "Praise be to God your Papa will be home soon," she said. "I have a few things to speak to him about."

Me too. I want to keep Big Jim and Adam. Maybe they'll change their minds about running away if they could stay with us. I'd feel better about going to Kentucky if we had them along.

She handed me the salve and some bandage strips, and I went behind the privacy blanket to apply it to my bruise in private.

A few minutes later, Papa entered wide-eyed. "Adam said Charlie almost drowned in the creek." He knelt beside Charlie and stroked his hair but didn't wake him.

I sniffled and explained. "I'm sorry. It was my fault."

"No." He rose and stood before Momma and me. "I'm the one to blame for this. I've neglected my family. Where are the others?"

"George has decided to add deer hunting to his chores." Momma's voice sounded curt. "Katie is with him. The younger girls are still foraging."

Papa looked at the floor. "I'll fetch them all in for lunch."

Hearing Momma's annoyance pleased me. *Maybe he'll stop his foolish ways and stay home.*

Chapter Nine

The voices of George and Katie mingled with Papa's out in the yard as the door opened. Lizzy, Susie, and Nancy entered with their baskets and mine, glancing at Charlie with tears in their eyes.

"Glad Charlie is all right," Lizzy said. "Adam told us what happened. We didn't know where you went."

George bounded inside, beaming, and hung the gun on the rack. "I shot a buck. Papa helped us skewer it for the spit."

Katie followed ahead of Papa, Big Jim, and Adam.

"Thanks to these men," Papa said, "we have two acres of hefty mounds ready for seedlings."

Big Jim and Adam smiled and nodded.

After we were seated, they took their place at the table. Papa sat back and cleared his throat. "I'll be taking Big Jim and Adam back to Mr. Thorndike after lunch. That way, I can put in a full day's work around here tomorrow."

I shook my head. "But we still need them. Please buy them from Mr. Thorndike."

Momma gasped, and Papa raised his brows.

"Yes, we want to keep them." George looked at Papa.

My siblings echoed enthusiasm. Momma intervened. "Settle down. This is something we cannot do."

"Why can't they be indentured and move to Kentucky with us, and then go free?" I asked.

Adam's jaw dropped, and Big Jim shifted in his chair. They watched Papa with big eyes.

Papa shook his head. "I wish it worked that way, but it doesn't. It's against the law in Virginia to set slaves free, and we can't afford them." His voice was calm.

I glared. "Adam saved Charlie's life. Isn't that worth defying British law?"

Big Jim and Adam gawked, along with my family.

Papa remained soft-spoken but sighed. "They have to go back. But we can reward them for their hard work." He retrieved his duffel bag from the corner, removed two gray wool blanket bundles, then handed one to Big Jim and one to Adam.

They unwrapped the blankets in their laps and sat staring. Each held a pipe and tobacco pouch, new moccasins, and two neatly folded linen shirts.

"I wanted you to have something for your hard work."

Big Jim folded the blanket around the gifts and placed it on the table. He squirmed in his seat, frowned at Papa, and shook his head. "Masta Thorndike won't like us to have these. He beat us if we accept. But this mighty kind of you, sir."

"How can he be so cruel?" My face grew hot as I sat back with my arms folded.

"Just not proper, miss." Adam lowered his eyes and returned the items.

"Take them, please," Papa said. "I'll make sure he knows you refused, but that I insisted." Papa smiled at Adam. "We are especially indebted to you for saving Charlie."

Adam grinned and took the gifts. "Thank you, Masta Shirley. I been pleased to work for your kind family and mighty glad the boy be safe."

Big Jim stared at the bundle before pulling it toward his chest as if it were some kind of treasure.

Papa nodded. "We'll tidy up the barn and hitch the wagon, then all can come say goodbye."

"Just lay the bedding on the wash table. We'll start on them in the morning," Momma said.

No one spoke as we worked, and too soon, we heard the creaking wagon pull in front of the cabin.

Big Jim held his hat in his hands, rubbing his thumb over its brim. I smiled at him. He cracked a smile and cleared his throat. "We enjoyed our time with you folks. Would be happy to come again if you needs us."

Adam frowned at him, then glanced down and eased toward the wagon.

Charlie lunged to the ground, grabbing Adam's ankles. "Stay."

"We don't belong to your papa." He squatted in front of Charlie. "We has to go back." He glanced at me as he stood. "But we stay if we could."

The way he said it, looking at me with desperation in his dark-brown eyes, set a lump in my throat. *He's going to run away.* My chest ached. *He's pleading for my continued silence.*

"Wait, I have to give you something." I rushed up to the loft and opened my linen box. I lifted the embroidered neckerchief with its tiny golden threads forming my initials and embellished with ivy, green tendrils and leaves. I'd spent hours working on it and daydreaming about my first dance. But the way things were going, I could make a new one sooner than I'd have a dance partner. And right now, Adam was deserving of it.

I scrambled down the ladder and placed the neckerchief in his hand. "I made this a few months back and want you to have it."

Adam's eyes widened, and he stepped back as if I'd handed him a snake. He tried to hand it back, shaking his head. "This too fine for me, miss."

"No, you need one, and I want you to know how special you are for saving Charlie."

He looked to Momma, then to Papa. They both smiled and nodded. Adam secured the white neckerchief around his dark neck. He smiled with bright white teeth that matched the bleached linen and tipped his hat. "This be mighty fine, miss. Thank you."

He and Big Jim climbed into the back of the wagon with their bundles.

Papa kissed Momma's cheek. "I'll teach Charlie how to swim when I get back." He climbed into the seat and shook the reins. Little Sis and General moved the rattling wagon forward.

I hugged the porch post and watched them round the curve out of sight as my eyes watered. *God make Adam and Big Jim change their minds about running away.*

The next instant, Momma said, "Well, children. It's best to get busy and not dwell on sorrow. We have over five hundred tobacco plants ready to go into two acres' worth of mounds. If we don't dawdle, we can set half before supper. Load the carts with 250 of the best seedlings."

I pushed away from the porch, wiping my face, and followed her.

"What about turning the meat?" George asked.

"Help us load the plants and tools, then you can stay and tend to it," Momma said.

When I saw the rows of perfect mounds created by Big Jim and Adam, a lump rose in my throat as irritation flooded in. *What a waste of labor for a now worthless crop. And why? Just so Papa can sit on the porch for an occasional smoke.* My ears burned for several seconds before I calmed down.

I pulled my cart to the first two rows and passed out hand shovels. My siblings, minus George, spread out, digging deep holes in each mound wide enough for the roots. I squatted up and down, placing the seedlings at the bottom while Katie raked in dirt to the leaf tops. Lizzy added a dipperful of water to set them. After two hours, my legs were wobbly and my back ached.

As I stood to stretch, Drummer jumped up, yapping. He rushed to Papa, who darted from behind a tree to play with him. *How can Papa be so happy after leaving Big Jim and Adam with that horrible man?*

"Mighty fine job, family." Papa scanned the field as Charlie and Sally scurried toward him. He scooped each one up and carried them like bundles of straw under his arms as they giggled. "Time to learn how to swim. Who's coming along to cool off in the creek?"

"Me," echoed my sisters.

"We have to avoid those yellow jackets, though," Katie said. "They're on this side of the bank beside the big oak tree."

Momma stared at Papa with big eyes as he approached.

He released the children and kissed her cheek, grinning. "I won't let them drown. I want to teach Sally how to hold her breath in the water, then I'll hand her off to Katie. Where's George?"

"Tending the venison," Momma said. "I'm going to lie down in the cabin a bit. I can't bear to watch. Bring my babies home in one piece."

He nodded at Momma. "Send George back with the fishing pole."

She waved and headed home. Lizzy and I followed her with rattling carts as the others clamored away with Papa.

When we reached the yard, Momma stopped at the fire pit. Lizzy and I continued to the barn, and George rushed in seconds later. He grabbed the cane pole and fishing gear, then waited for Lizzy in the yard. She glanced back at me. "Are you coming?"

"No. Not in the mood." I crumpled my apron, wiping my sweaty hands.

She shrugged and followed George.

On my way out, I glimpsed the corner where the men had slept, and my eyes watered.

Momma moved the meat from the fire pit to cool and stared at me, tilting her head.

"I don't feel like playing," I said. "Thought I'd work on the mending."

A slight grin accompanied her nod as she led the way inside. "Fretting about troubles is exhausting. All we can do is pray and wait sometimes. Everything comes out in the wash."

I scowled behind her back. *Plenty of things don't come out in the wash.* But I prayed for Charlie and Sally for Momma's sake, and Big Jim and Adam for my own.

As Momma pulled her coverlet back and lay down, I sat in the rocker, lifted a shirt being made for George, and found the needle weaved into the side seam. Sewing relaxed me, but once both sides were basted, I grew bored. George would have to try the garment on before the final stitches could be made. I set it aside and glanced at the counter where Papa had placed the *Virginia Gazette*, along with other documents.

Tiptoeing to prevent the floorboards from creaking, I sifted through the pile and eased out the *Gazette*. As it slid free, a folded letter bearing the signature of Colonel William Preston landed on my foot. One kick would land it in the fireplace, but I lifted it to my hand, staring at the offending name.

Momma faced the wall, breathing in soft rhythms. Unfolding the letter might wake her. *No, I dare not.* I scanned the exposed portion above the signature instead.

...These incidents have caused much fear, and loyalists all over Virginia are incurring the wrath of the Whigs. Reverend Brown has informed me that three naval ships of marines are on the way to Virginia to keep order.

My chest tightened. I read again, interpreting. *Loyalists are incurring the wrath of those who want separation from England. What kind of wrath? What if Papa's discovered?*

No longer in the mood to read, I returned the post and the letter into the stack, then stepped onto the porch. The door creaked closed as I sucked in a deep breath before sitting.

As the afternoon shadows lengthened across the yard, Drummer trotted up to me and piled into my lap, dripping wet. I wrapped my arms around his smelly body, raising him into a hug. He was my last link to normal, and I didn't want to let go.

The chatter and laughter of my siblings emerging from the woods soon after preceded Charlie running into the yard, wild-eyed and loud. His bushy hair had dried, matted. "I swim three times."

Momma burst outside and squatted to embrace him. "I'm so proud of you." Then she stood and reached for Sally.

Papa handed her off with a smile. "She did well. Even learned to roll to her back and stay afloat. But it took me near thirty minutes to convince Charlie there was no serpent in the creek. Maybe he saw one slither away from the tree roots."

I chuckled. "No, sir. Adam told him that story to keep him from going near it again. Guess it worked."

Charlie clapped his hands and chanted, "No serpent."

Momma sent Sally inside, then stooped to hold Charlie's chin. "Nonetheless, stay away from that creek unless someone big is with you."

He nodded and added, "Ma'am."

"Are there fish to fry?" Momma stood but staggered sideways and steadied herself with the post.

Papa didn't seem to notice, but I rose beside her, worried.

"Yes, ma'am," Papa said. "George and Katie are cleaning them now. Good-sized trout. Are you all right?"

"Stood too fast, is all."

His brow furrowed. "I'm sorry you've had to shoulder my share of the work on the place. Maybe it's been too much."

Momma stepped back, cutting her eyes at Papa. "Rue the day that I'm too weak to feather my nest."

He grinned and tipped his hat. "My apologies, ma'am. I'll take a ride with Lizzy and break Big Red's rebellious streak."

Momma smiled, raising her chin. "Supper will be ready in an hour or so."

I released Drummer to follow Papa and Lizzy to the barn and went to the spring to scrub the mud from my petticoat. George emerged from the barn toting a bucket of fish entrails into the woods, and Katie brought the gutted fish, threaded on twine, to the spring. Seemed to be a good dozen.

"Sure sad we couldn't keep Big Jim and Adam," she said. "Why didn't you come back with George? It was nice to sit on the bank and dangle our feet."

Touched that she missed me, I stayed to chat while she dipped the string of fish in the water and flicked off the remaining innards.

"I needed to be away from Papa's happiness," I said.

She tilted her head and grinned. "What?"

I shrugged. "I'm upset with him about...well, a lot of things, and when he came back happy and singing, it annoyed me."

Katie stood with the dripping fish, frowning and shaking her head. "I like it when Papa is happy. It means everything is going to be all right. Maybe you worry too much. I'm taking these to Momma." She stepped around me and went inside.

Her words annoyed me. I had knowledge she didn't have, but it was my own fault. If I had left Papa's saddlebags and secret box alone, I would be blissfully ignorant too.

Chapter Ten

As I left the barn, Drummer pranced into the yard from the creek trail. Papa rode in, towing Big Red with Lizzy atop, cradling her left arm in a sling made from her apron.

I rushed to them. "What's happened?"

Lizzy grimaced. "Big Red balked at the creek crossing and reared. I slid off fine, but my foot slipped on a slimy place in the water, and I landed on a big rock."

"Bruised, but nothing broken. It will mend in a day or two." Papa dismounted, then eased her from the horse.

I glanced back at Lizzy. "I'm sorry you're hurt."

She nodded and went to the cabin.

Papa handed me the defiant horse's long rein. "I need you to trade horses with Lizzy. Patriot will suit her better."

"What?" I stepped back. "Trade?"

He nodded. "Big Red needs a firm hand to break his rebellious streak before the trip. Let's go straighten him out." Papa's eyes softened. He lifted my hand to his lips for a light kiss. "Best not get attached to horses—remember."

Still reeling from the shock, I glared into Big Red's eye. "You're mine now, and you will mind me." I mounted and urged him forward.

Papa followed on Little Sis.

Big Red obeyed every command I gave him without hesitation until he balked at the creek. I slapped his hindquarters with my long rein and shouted, "Walk." He bounded into the water, stumbled over a few rocks, and climbed the bank on the other side. I rubbed his neck. "Good boy. Now, no more of your shenanigans." I scratched him behind the ears, and he calmed.

Papa laughed. "That's what I thought. He's a good horse. Just too spirited for Lizzy. William McGuire said he's fast. He considered keeping him for racing but didn't have time to work with him. He knows who his master is now. Come on back."

The horse crossed more surefooted. "May I take him to the clearing and let him run? He's bursting with energy. I think it will help him settle down."

Papa grinned and nodded. "I suppose we have time. I'm curious to see just what he's been holding back."

When we reached the clearing, Big Red's head bobbed. I made him stand still. "I'll release you when I'm ready, Rebel." I smiled and stroked his neck. "Yes, that's your new name." I fixed my feet in the stirrups, gripped him with my thighs, then lightened my grip and yelled, "Yah!"

He accelerated so fast I couldn't breathe and had to rein him into a wide circle to slow him to a trot.

Papa galloped toward me shouting, "Whew, he's fast. Were you frightened?" He halted beside us. "We'd better not tell Momma I let you do that. She'll flog me for sure. We just might have us a good racehorse."

"My heart's still pounding." I blew out a breath. "I like him. I won't say a word to Momma. I might have been halfway to Kentucky before nightfall."

"Not without me." He chuckled. "We better get home."

The ride exhilarated me enough to smile as Papa hummed the frog courting song all the way to the barn.

"Will you unsaddle and groom Little Sis?" he asked. "I want to slice the venison for Momma."

"Yes sir." I dismounted and walked the horses in.

As I finished grooming, Lizzy came in with her arm in a sling. "Sorry you have to trade but thank you." She rubbed Patriot's neck.

I hung up the currycomb and stroked Lizzy's back. "To tell you the truth, I don't mind. Something about his spirit suits me." I smiled. "And I've changed his name to Rebel."

She laughed. "That's perfect. Glad you're not upset."

"How's your arm?"

"Sore, but Momma put a poultice on it and made me drink some willow tea."

Drummer's furious barking startled us. As we stepped into the yard, a dozen or more angry-looking men led by Mr. Thorndike rode in.

Papa covered the meat he was slicing on the wash table with a clean cloth and wiped his hands with a damp rag. He snapped his fingers to heel Drummer and motioned for me and Lizzy to get inside.

Momma stepped to the doorway. "Get in here," she told us.

My heart raced as Papa greeted the men without smiling.

I backed into the cabin on wobbly legs.

George reached for a gun from the rack, but Momma stayed his arm and scowled.

"No. These men are our neighbors." She allowed the door to remain open, but I moved to the window.

"Why are they mad at Papa?" Katie asked.

Momma didn't answer.

I glared at Katie and held a finger to my lips, easing the shutters open so I could hear. Papa stood firm as the men circled around him. Mr. Thorndike dismounted and pointed in Papa's face, shouting, "I accuse you of loyalism and inciting my slaves to run."

A cold rush went through me, and my family gasped.

Papa took a step back. "Why do you accuse me of such a thing, sir?" He sounded edgy.

I held my breath. *Don't hit him, Papa.*

Mr. Thorndike snarled like a wild animal. "Soon as you left my men in the shanty, they lit out. By the time my foreman noticed, half an hour had passed. Witnesses say you gave them blankets, shoes, and shirts. They also say loyalists in these parts are encouraging slaves to join the Regulars in Williamsburg. Now, lie to my face and say you didn't entice them to run."

Papa's head jerked. "I gave them those as a reward for their hard work and for saving my son from drowning." He turned to the gathered men. "But I assure you, gentlemen—I am innocent of the charge of incitement."

A man I didn't know addressed Papa. "Why are you still working under the loyalist Colonel Preston, making surveys under British laws instead of those authorized by the Assembly of Virginia?"

Before Papa could answer, Mr. Thorndike stepped into his face again. "Well, I say you are a scheming loyalist, and we're going to burn you out. Remove your family from the cabin."

As men began dismounting, I rushed into the yard, shouting, "No. Please."

I crumpled to my knees in front of Mr. Thorndike. "Papa didn't know. I heard Big Jim tell Adam to hush about running away. He didn't want to get Papa in trouble with you." I caught my breath. "I didn't say anything because Big Jim prevented the escape." Staggering to my feet, I wiped my wet face and stared into Mr. Thorndike's eyes. "Sir, it's my fault, and I'm sorry." Heaving breaths, I glanced around at the men who displayed shocked faces. "Please, don't burn us out."

Papa pulled me away from Mr. Thorndike and wrapped me in his arms while I sobbed.

One of the men in the group yelled, "Leave them be, men. No call to ruin the family. The man's been warned. Let's go."

I peeked over Papa's arm as the men remounted. Mr. Thorndike glared down at Papa. "I demand compensation." He turned his horse toward the road.

Papa remained silent.

Horses snorted. Hoofs beat the ground, then faded as the men departed. Papa took a deep breath, continuing to cuddle me to his chest. His heart raced in my ear. He whispered, "It's over. Go inside. I'll finish the meat."

My stomach churned as he handed me off to Momma. Once inside, I grabbed the scrap bucket and threw up.

Momma applied a wet cloth to my forehead. "Sit here and calm down." She stroked my back.

George stood watch at the window. "I can't believe Papa let those men curse him like that. Why, I would have—"

"Hush this minute, George Michael Shirley," Momma snapped. "Your Papa's cool head kept him from being shot. We need him more than a cabin or barn." Momma went to her rocker and sat, wiping her face.

"Sorry, Momma." George closed the shutter.

I climbed into a chair at the table and lay my head down, sobbing.

The door creaked closed, and Papa's boot steps thudded toward the table. Chairs scooted across the floor as the family settled at the table. I raised my head, drying my face.

Nancy sniffled. "Why did those bad men come?"

Papa sat forward, resting folded arms on the table. "They're not bad men, just angry, because Big Jim and Adam ran away from Mr. Thorndike, and the men thought they came back here. We're safe now."

"But why did they run away?" Lizzy shook her head and dabbed her eyes with her apron.

"Slaves have been promised freedom if they escape and join the king's regiments against the independent militias."

"What?" George jumped to his feet.

"What's freedom?" Susie asked.

George sat back down and waited for Papa's reply.

I rocked in anguish. *What if he did help them escape? What if they are hiding in the barn now?* Tears rolled down my cheeks as he spoke.

"Freedom means being able to choose where to live and what to do. It also means being able to have a say in matters that affect your choices. But slavery is a complicated matter." Papa sighed. "Some regard their slaves as nothing more than livestock. But if you mistreat any living thing in your care, it will want to flee from you."

"Were Big Jim and Adam mistreated?" Katie sniffled.

"I think so." He nodded.

Gasps echoed around the table. Momma's chair creaked as she rocked faster.

"What will happen if they're caught?" I choked on the words.

Papa sat at the table, folding his hands around mine. "They will be returned to Mr. Thorndike and, most likely, beaten."

Tears welled in my eyes as I pulled my hands from him. I broke out in a sweat as I stood and glared at Papa.

He tilted his head and frowned.

I ignored my family's stares. "But if they join the regulars, they will surely be put in the front lines. We could have bought them from Mr. Thorndike and kept them safe until the British are defeated. Maybe the slave laws will change and allow them to go free. I hate loyalists."

My heart raced, and my hands trembled. *I just told Papa I hated him to his face. Now what?* "I'm sorry for my outburst. May I please be excused? I'm not hungry."

"Yes, you may." Papa's calm tone made me shiver.

The silence that followed me into the loft was like the eerie stillness before a storm.

Chapter Eleven

After a slow descent from the loft in the morning, I glanced at the table where Papa sat snuggling Nancy in his lap. He stood, placed her in a chair, and motioned for me to follow him outside. My heart pounded, mortified at the possibility of being switched at my age. *Be strong.*

He stopped mid-yard and faced me with glistening eyes. "I can deal with you hating me." His voice quavered. "There's a lot going on that I can't explain at the moment. But don't disrespect me again."

"I don't hate you, but I'm ashamed of you." My stomach fluttered, anticipating his command to get a switch from the bush and meet him at the woodshed.

His gaze drifted to the ground as he shook his head and grimaced. "I'm sorry you feel that way." He glanced at me as he walked toward the barn. "Tell everyone to meet me in the tobacco field after breakfast. We need to hoe before it rains. I'll eat later."

"Yes, sir." I bowed my head, amazed at avoiding a spanking, but the sadness in his eyes pricked me.

A stray tear dribbled down my cheek as I walked away. *But I had to say it.* I sighed and gazed into the threatening gray clouds accumulating in the southwest sky. *At least the neighbors won't come back if it rains.* I wiped my cheek and opened the door. Papa hadn't denied the loyalist charge, only that he had nothing to do with inciting Big Jim and Adam to escape. *But what if the neighbors discover he's a traitor? We're still in danger.*

Stares from my family seared my heart. I cleared my throat. "Papa's gone to the field. We're to join him after we eat. We have to get the hoeing done before it rains."

"Sit then," Momma said. She led the blessing and concluded with, "And may there be peace between neighbors and kin. Amen. Now, eat quickly."

We joined Papa soon after, spreading out along the rows, removing weeds, and rebuilding the hills around the foot-high plants. Thunder rumbled across the sky from the distant ridgeline into the valley. But I finished my row and wiped sweat from my brow.

"Load your hoes in the cart and let's get inside. Those clouds will drop rain within the hour." Papa lifted Charlie, took Nancy's hand, and went to help Momma.

George pushed the wheelbarrow up to me and whispered, "I think Papa's doing something wrong."

My breath caught as I peered at him and then at the family ahead of us.

He kicked a rock before continuing, "That box is back in the barn loft. I tried to read one of the letters. All I made out is that a man named Connolly freed some Indian prisoners. They are going to tell other Indians to stay loyal to King George and fight the rebels. But someone from Wood's Fort is going to stop them. Papa is supposed to get word to Cook's Fort about it." He peered into my eyes.

My gut churned. I shook my head. "I don't know what Papa is up to but stop snooping in his business. It only makes us worry more, and there's nothing we can do about it, anyway." I dropped my hoe in the wheelbarrow and rushed away from him. *How can Papa be part of inciting the Indians to fight us?*

As we entered the yard, Papa was off to the side of the barn, speaking to a man hidden behind a tall red bay. No matter which way I tilted my head, the view was blocked.

Inside the barn, we hung the hoes and dumped dirt from the wheelbarrow, then peeked through the slats.

"Hey, I think that's the man Papa spoke to before. That night I sneaked around to the side of the barn," George said.

"How can you tell?" I smirked. "It was dark outside."

"Same size and wears his hair the same way."

I glimpsed black hair tied back in a simple pigtail but couldn't see his face. He was slightly taller than Papa.

The man and Papa moved closer to the woodpile, further from our sight.

A strong gust of wind shook the trees and swirled the dirt in the barn. "We better get inside," I said.

"Wish I could be a fly on his horse and hear what they're saying," George said as he headed into the cabin.

I followed but glanced back at the men twice before reaching the porch and going inside.

"Who's that?" I asked.

Momma looked up from snapping beans. "Young Mr. McGuire."

My heart fluttered as I pushed a shutter back to watch them.

Katie eased close to my ear and whispered, "I saw him ride in. He's quite handsome, but Momma wouldn't let me stare."

He needs to be warned about Papa.

"Girls, come away from the window," Momma said.

Katie obeyed.

Now or never. "May I please go outside and meet Mr. McGuire? I want to thank him for the horses."

"No. You may not." Momma frowned. "Now, mind me."

I closed the shutter but stared at the gray slats.

Momma stood with the bowl. "Mary Ann Shirley. I'll not tell you again."

Hang the consequences. With a racing heart, I sprinted out the door, but lost my nerve and leapt from the porch, ducking behind the wood stack. *What am I doing? I can't betray Papa.* Panting, I sneaked behind a tree, close enough to listen. *At least I can know what they're saying.*

"Aye, sir. Only small parties of Cherokee hunters about." Young McGuire's baritone brogue intrigued me. "One confirmed Dunmore's involvement with Connolly himself."

Papa cleared his throat. "Maybe things will calm down soon. Thank you again for the horses."

It seemed an abrupt change of subject. I held my breath. *Did he see me?*

"You're welcome, and how's that fast sorrel working out? You want to trade him for one more mild?" Mr. McGuire asked.

Papa chuckled. "He's feisty, but my eldest daughter settled him down."

Heat spread across my face at the mention.

"Well, now." Mr. McGuire's hearty laugh made me smile. "Let himself be tamed by a girl, did he?"

"Yes, sir." Papa's voice boomed. "Both stubborn as all get out and high-strung to boot. Do you need refreshment? We have plenty of hoecakes."

I held my breath. *Please say no. How will I explain being outside? Momma is sure to send me straight to bed as soon as I set foot in the door.*

"No, sir, but thank you kindly. I hope to make Fort Cook before that storm flails me."

I exhaled slowly, and my stomach relaxed.

"Stay safe out there," Papa said.

"Thank you, sir. Good day to you and your family."

I dared a peek around the tree to see William McGuire's back as his horse trotted up the east road and disappeared into the woods. Looking back to the yard, I watched Papa remove a letter from his hunting shirt, read it, then head to the barn. He tipped his hat to Momma, who had stepped onto the porch and sat on the edge, scanning the area—most likely for me.

I took a deep breath, stood straight, and emerged from behind the tree. *I'm in so much trouble.*

Momma crossed her arms and narrowed her eyes as I approached. "What possessed you to do such a thing?" Her voice cracked.

"I'm sorry." I sat, wrapping my arms around her neck, sniffling.

She snuggled my head. "What's going on? This isn't like you at all."

The shutters creaked behind me, but I didn't care if my siblings heard. I stood and faced her. Seven months of turmoil spilled out. "I don't understand why Papa risks our lives by remaining a loyalist and betraying our neighbors. Why do you allow it?"

She gasped.

I continued, "It's not fair to endanger us and make us leave everything behind. I don't want to move to Kentucky Territory. I want Papa to stand with the patriots for new laws. I want to stay here." I pointed to the ground. With a deep breath, I sat beside her again, burying my face in my apron. "Why hasn't God changed Papa's mind?"

The cabin door creaked open, and Charlie blurted, "Mary, nap."

"Shh," Katie hushed him. "Sorry, he got away from me."

"Put Charlie and Sally down for naps, then you and Lizzy gather the diapers to wash."

"Yes, ma'am," Katie said. The door closed, and feet scrambled behind it.

Momma turned, pulling me into her arms, and rocked me until I calmed down. Then she raised my chin. "These are questions you must resolve. They require trust. If you can't trust Papa at this time, at least trust God to take care of us. You can't live here alone, and I can't fix this for you. I'm scared too. There will be many challenges ahead, but we must remain strong for each other." She stroked my hair and kissed my wet cheek. "We all have bad days. The important thing is to work through the anger so you don't become bitter. Bitterness is neither helpful nor productive. I forgive your defiant act this time, but consequences must follow future rebellion."

"Yes, ma'am. I'm sorry." But bitterness had already taken root, and its tentacles ran deep.

I laid my head on Momma's shoulder until Papa walked Little Sis from the barn. "Is everything all right?" He frowned.

Momma stood, wiping her cheeks.

Papa held up his letter. "This is from Colonel Preston, explaining the survey conflict and his position as survey general. I'm taking it to Mr. Thorndike, so he'll simmer down."

"Maybe you should wait a day. He's too angry now." Momma stepped into his arms.

They embraced a moment, before Papa stepped back, smiling. "He'll be all right as soon as he reads this. Oh. William McGuire shared some pumpkin seeds. Need them planted before it rains. I left them on a barrel in the barn. I'll be back soon."

After mounting, he smiled at me and waved, but I scowled and turned my back.

Momma noticed. Her eyes narrowed, and her tone sharpened. "Maybe time alone in the garden planting the pumpkin seeds will tame your rebellious heart. There is a nice spot in the northeast corner, on the other side of the squash."

"Storm's coming in." I frowned and checked the drooping gray clouds.

"Then you should hurry." She walked past me and closed the door with a thud.

Count it all joy when you face trials of many kinds. The Bible verse popped into my head as I walked to the barn, but I wasn't in the mood to change my attitude.

Seeing the small linen bag on the barrel only made my chest hurt. *I'm a coward like Papa. Why didn't I speak to William? Now, here I am planting his pumpkin seeds, while Papa is off defending himself.*

I snatched the bag and my hoe, then hurried down the trail to the garden. The pumpkins wouldn't be ready for harvesting until October, but someone would enjoy steaming and roasting them, making pies, and using them as lanterns. The ground needed some extra work but hacking into the soil eased my foul mood. As I dropped the seeds into the shallow trenches, wind whipped my petticoat around my ankles, and a light rain fell. I raked dirt over the seeds and trudged back to the yard with muddy feet.

The fresh scent of rain followed me into the barn. I hung the hoe on a peg, then climbed into the loft and parted the shutters so the breeze could drift in. I lay back on the crunchy hay, not ready to face my family.

A loud thump startled me awake, and Katie yelled, "Are you going to live in the barn or come inside with the family? Supper's ready."

"Coming." I sat up and scooted to the edge.

When I peered down, Katie wasn't there, but Little Sis was back in her stall. *I didn't hear Papa come in.* I climbed down the ladder and sloshed through the mud, dreading a reprimand from Papa.

My family stared as I removed my bonnet and hung it on the peg next to Katie's wet one. "I'm sorry. I dozed off." In trouble anyway, I took a deep breath as I sat in my chair and asked, "What did William McGuire want?"

Papa raised his eyebrows and smirked. "You heard him ask me about Rebel and my accurate description of the high-strung, stubborn daughter who tamed him."

Katie snorted, and the others snickered.

I cleared my throat and dared another topic. "He also said something about Governor Dunmore, and someone named Connolly."

George glared at me, but quickly looked at his plate.

"That he did." Papa's tone remained controlled. "However, that is a private matter. I can say that Lord Dunmore and his family need our prayers at this time. His removal of the powder the day after the attacks in the Colony of Massachusetts has added to the uproar." He pierced my heart with a sharp, squinting glare. "Now, no more rebellion from you. My patience is running thin, and honor and respect for your parents will be restored willingly or by force."

"Yes, sir." I bowed my head, compliant while he prayed, but tuned out his blessing of Lord Dunmore.

Chapter Twelve

Momma sat on the side of her bed and blew out a breath. She had spent most of the morning in bed, queasy, and, without mentioning it, I knew she was expecting a baby. My siblings seemed to turn up every two years, and Sally had turned a year-old back in March. But this baby was making her sicker than usual. Bouts of nausea had come on every morning since Papa left on a month-long survey job, a few days after William McGuire's visit at the end of May. The month had spilled over into July.

Katie and I took turns cooking outside and delegating duties to the younger children. But this morning a dispute arose over what to do in the tobacco field now that the cutworms had been conquered and whose turn it was to check traps with George. We looked to Momma to resolve it.

"It's time for the first tobacco topping," she said, "and Katie's turn to go with George. Lizzy can take the littles to the garden for carrots and peas. Check the corn silks and let me know if they're brown." She moaned and lay back down.

Lizzy took Sally and Charlie by the hand and left for the garden. George and Katie gathered the bullets and powder horn, then called Drummer as they bounded out the door.

I laid my gun on the ground before entering a row of waist-high tobacco plants. Susie helped me snip off the white trumpet-shaped flower pods that were just beginning to open into soft pink petals. Removing them allowed the leaves to grow larger. I instructed Nancy in pinching off the small sucker leaves at the bottom of each plant.

As I neared the tree line, an eerie sense of being watched made the hair on the back of my neck prickle. Ever since George told me about Papa's letter and the Indians staying loyal to the king, fear of raids worried me. But William McGuire mentioned seeing only passing Cherokee hunters.

A tree branch cracked—leaves shuffled. I backed in the direction of my rifle, watching and wishing I had

Drummer with me. A second later, a rabbit bounced into the open, saw me, and dashed back into the shrubs.

Before my nerves settled back down, gunshots crackled from the northern ridge where Katie and George were.

Susie and Nancy looked to me.

No reason to be concerned. I shook my head. "Probably just a coon in the trap."

A second shot stole my breath. *What are they doing?* "Let's get to the barn, and I'll go check on them." Shouldering my gun, I pulled the cart at a quick pace with its contents rattling.

I abandoned the cart in the barn for Susie and Nancy to unload and heaved the saddle over Rebel's back. "Tell Momma I've gone to check on them." I sheathed the gun and mounted.

Clicking my tongue, I urged Rebel into a trot, then allowed him free rein to run to the narrow creek trail before slowing to a canter. At the creek, I yelled, "Hey. Where are you?"

"Over here." George waved from a thicket on the other side of the creek. "Katie shot a bear."

Blood drained from my head. Rebel eased into the water, splashed surefooted across, and climbed the bank. Still in a stupor, I dismounted and draped the reins over a bush. "Good boy. Stay."

Previously parted vines and broken branches led to a grassy clearing where Katie sat on the ground, hugging her knees, heaving breaths as she cried. A strong musky stench emanated from a large black bear a few feet from her.

George poked it with the stock of the rifle. "I don't know why you're upset. You shot a bear all by yourself. Papa and Momma will be proud."

As I emerged, Drummer peered at me, wagging his tail, then went back to lapping a puddle of blood next to the bear's head.

"The bear was eating a coon it had ripped out of the trap." George beamed. "It lunged toward us, and Katie shot him right in the heart. Papa will be amazed."

"But I heard two shots." I frowned.

"That was mine." He cradled the barrel in the crook of his arm and approached. "Wanted to make sure it was dead."

I sighed and shook my head. "Take Rebel home, tell Momma what's happened, and bring the knives. We'll have to butcher it here—it's too heavy for us to lift to the horse. And take Drummer. I can't watch him do that anymore."

"I'll hitch Gideon to the wagon and come as far as I can." He retrieved the rabbits taken from previous traps and tore through the brambles to the trail.

I squatted in front of Katie. "Can you stand now?"

"I'll try." She sniffled and rose to her feet, holding my arm. After taking two steps, she stopped. "I'm dizzy."

"Take a deep breath; maybe you're in shock. Do you need to sit again, big bear hunter?" I teased, to lighten her mood.

"No, I'll just stand still a minute. I can't believe I shot a bear." She let go of my arm and appeared steady on her feet.

I stepped cautiously toward the animal, waving off flies, then stooped and ruffled its coarse black fur before holding my breath and rushing back to Katie. "I've never seen one up close before, but the smell is worse than Drummer when he's wet. Maybe Papa will let you keep the pelt. I'd say you earned the rights to it."

"I don't want the smelly thing." She wrinkled her nose and turned her head toward the rattling sounds of our wagon.

"Let's widened the path for Momma." I grabbed a stick and lifted brambles from the trail as Katie followed behind, tamping them back with a larger branch.

At the crossing, we watched Momma and George unload the carts from the wagon box, then wade across the creek. Momma rushed to Katie with outstretched arms. "My stars, are you all right?"

Katie stepped into her arms. "Yes, ma'am, just shaken."

"I'm going to need your help now." Momma pulled back and looked into her eyes. "Are you able?"

She nodded, then Momma turned to George. "Give me the skinning knife and bring the clean canvas. We need to get this done as soon as possible. I've had to leave Lizzy managing the littles." She bent over the bear, gagging several times. "Let's get this bear rolled over."

We grabbed handfuls of black fur and pulled until the belly was exposed. Momma lifted its front paw and slid the knife under the skin. She sliced straight to its elbow, across the chest, and up the other arm to the paw. The hindquarters were next, followed by a cut straight up the belly from the vent to the chest.

As she fleshed the hide from the carcass, Katie and I placed a clean canvas under the exposed meat. I took the butcher knife and removed the legs at the joints, and Katie did the arms. Momma sliced the bacon away from the ribs and cut the back portions off. The whole process took a couple of hours. When we'd finished, the fur was folded, and the meat was wrapped in the canvas.

"I'll be back in a minute." I went into a clump of nearby bushes and relieved myself. As I emerged, a near-naked Indian darted past a tree a few yards away. My breath caught. I rushed out

to Momma.

"What's wrong?" she asked.

My heart raced, and I felt myself trembling. "There's an Indian out there."

Momma grabbed the gun from the tree and aimed toward the woods.

"Hush that kind of talk. You're scaring me," Katie said.

Momma frowned. "Are you sure?"

I swallowed. "Yes. He was close enough to attack, but ran away. Maybe he's a passing hunter like William McGuire saw."

"Keep watch while Katie and I haul the meat across." Momma handed the weapon to me.

When they finished, I waded out, careful of the slippery places. I made it up the bank and climbed into the wagon box. Momma and I held rifles toward the creek.

"Gideon, *waalk*." George drew out the command the way Papa taught him and drove us home.

As we pulled into the yard, Lizzy rushed to Katie. "Were you scared?"

"Terrified."

Momma interrupted, "We'll take turns on guard until Papa gets home to check on things. George is first. Now, the rest of us have to get this hide and meat salted down. We'll cut the fat from the meat for grease and slice it for jerky. It's going to be tedious, so let's get to it."

By late afternoon, the yard was filled with the savory smells of hickory smoke as strips of bear meat dangled from the rack that straddled the smoldering fire. No longer concerned about Indians, I squatted beside the cooking pit, frying the last slice of bear bacon as George returned from his hourly walk around the perimeter of the yard with the rifle. There'd been no other sightings.

Drummer yelped and wagged his tail.

Relief swept through me, and my stomach fluttered with joy. "It's Papa." In spite of not wanting to, I'd missed him. And fear of Indians roaming our land still unnerved me.

Little Sis sauntered into the yard with Papa waving and helloing. "I've been smelling bacon for at least a mile." He dismounted and stooped down to rub Drummer's belly, then reached for me. I smiled and stepped into his hug before moving back to the fire pit.

"Where did bacon come from?" He sniffed the air. "Smells like bear."

I nodded. "Katie shot one this morning."

His forehead furrowed in confusion. "What? Little Katie?"

"She'll tell you about it. But I—"

My tale of the Indian was interrupted by shouts of "Papa's home" as my siblings swarmed him with greetings. When George approached, I held a finger to my lips, indicating, *don't tell him about the Indian yet.*

He nodded and shook Papa's hand before hugging him. "Are you finished with road surveys?"

"Yes. I have a few more jobs for some individuals, but I'll be home for a few days."

"Good, because—" George glanced at me, then at the ground.

Papa peered toward the cabin. "Where's Momma?"

"Resting," Lizzy said. "She was sick this morning and dizzy this afternoon from all the butchering work."

Papa frowned and handed George Little Sis's lead rope. "Take care of my horse so I can check on Momma."

George headed to the barn, and Papa took a strip of bacon on his way into the cabin.

After moving the hot skillet to a flat rock to cool, I carried the platter of bacon inside, placed it on the table, and glanced toward Momma. Papa sat on the bed, stroking her head. He whispered in German, *"Mein liebchen,"* and kissed her lips. She cuddled his hand to her cheek with her eyes closed. Mine watered.

She whispered in his ear, and by the way his head jerked back, I figured she mentioned the Indian.

"One day at a time," he said and helped her stand.

She held on to his arm all the way to the table and sat. "Thank you, girls, for taking over."

Papa opened the door. "Come on in now, Son."

George removed his hat and hung the rifle on the rack. "Did Mary tell you about the Indian she saw?"

"Indian?" Susie turned her head toward me.

"Just a passing hunter." Papa sat at the table holding a finger to his lips. "Now, I want to hear about Katie's bear."

Katie blushed and told her tale.

After supper, Papa carried his chair to the porch with his pipe between his lips and motioned for me to follow him outside. He sat puffing beechnut-scented smoke from one corner of his mouth.

"Tell me about the Indian you saw."

"He was skinny and painted red, wearing a loincloth with no breeches. Bald-headed except for a spiked strip down the middle."

Papa frowned. "Could be Cherokee. Where was Drummer?"

"Home. Had to keep him away while we butchered the bear. I remembered Mr. McGuire saying they were mostly out hunting, so I tried not to be scared."

He nodded.

I hoped he would say there was nothing to worry about, but he sucked on his pipe with his brows still kinked, staring at the yard. His silence unnerved me.

"May I speak with you?"

He smiled and removed his pipe to speak. "Are you going to be nice?"

I nodded my intention and smiled.

"Are the Indians remaining loyal to the British? How will they know which of us are loyalist? Will they raid again?"

Papa studied my face, then sighed. "Governor Dunmore has been encouraging slaves to revolt and the Shawnee to attack settlers west of the Appalachians. He fled Williamsburg with his family three days ago. Trouble is coming. The Ohio tribes don't care to distinguish who's loyal or not. They want to force us out for good." Papa puffed on the pipe. "But scouts say we're in no danger at present."

"But how do you know these things? I want to know the truth about everything."

He shifted in his chair as if suddenly uncomfortable. He lowered his pipe, glanced at me, then flicked tobacco flakes off his knee. "I hear news while I'm out surveying."

He just lied to me. I folded my arms across my chest and glared. "Surveying? I know about your survey jobs. I've read your hidden documents. How can you be a traitor to our patriot neighbors?" Spewing my knowledge into the open gave me a sense of peace. I lowered my arms, ready to receive whatever punishment he deemed necessary.

His head jerked back with a frown as he whispered, "Traitor?"

The hurt behind his eyes sent pangs of guilt to my chest.

He took a deep breath. "You know too much but lack understanding." His calm tone deepened my regret. He stood and took my hand, squinting into my eyes. "I can't explain anything." His jaw clenched, and his eyes widened. "It's too dangerous. Please, leave my papers alone and trust me."

His stare deepened.

I swallowed but didn't commit.

He stepped back, releasing my hand. "Maybe you'll be proud of me again one day."

My silent *I want to be* ended with a sigh.

"Good night then." He took a draw from his pipe and returned to his chair.

I stooped to his cheek and kissed it, blinking tears. "Good night."

Chapter Thirteen

Corn harvest officially ended the last Saturday of July as I vigorously shook the remaining grit from my petticoat, circulating what little air there was. Ten large canvas bags of dried, hulled corn for milling and seed were packed away in barrels to stay dry. Papa also filled twenty small canvas bags for the trip to Kentucky.

I wiped sweat from my brow and joined Momma and Lizzy at the spring to splash water on my face and neck. After drinking dipperfuls of cold water from the barrel, I poured one down Lizzy's back. She squealed, and I stood still while she doused me. The others joined in as they filed out of the barn.

Drummer stared toward the southern end of the yard, sniffing. He glanced at Papa but didn't bark. "Good boy," Papa said. "Sit."

A young man rounded the corner on a sleek bay, and there I stood, dripping wet like a child, hoping it wasn't William McGuire. To my relief, the man's clothes indicated someone more official. He wore a fancy side-folded hat, a gold shirt offset by a dark-blue waistcoat with brass buttons, and tan breeches.

When he skidded to a stop, dirt blew into our faces. I shielded my eyes in the crook of my arm as he addressed Papa without dismounting. "Are you Michael Shirley?"

Fear shot through me.

"I am." Papa stepped closer.

I lowered my arm as the man made a mark in a small notebook. He unfurled a document, and read, "In accordance with the newly passed Militia Act of July seventeenth, in the year of our Lord 1775, Botetourt County Lieutenant Colonel Andrew Lewis hereby orders that all able-bodied men sixteen to fifty muster at Camp Pleasant by the first day of September. Failure to muster will carry a fine of three shillings. Exemptions from conscription will be considered at that time." He rolled the document and placed it in his knapsack, then looked at Papa. "Sir, please raise your right hand to indicate you've heard and understand these instructions."

Papa did so.

The man made another mark, tipped his fancy side-folded hat, and cantered along the western trail and out of sight.

Momma held on to the fence rail, her eyes wide and her jaw clenched. But I smiled. *Now he'll have to stay. No going to Kentucky now.*

He rushed past me, taking Momma into his arms. "Don't worry. These are just preparations. But this does put a rush on things."

My temples throbbed as I steamed. *What? How can he refuse?*

She stepped back and took a deep breath. "What now?"

"I have an important survey job to do for a man down near Wood's Fort before we leave, which means heading out after lunch. I'm going to take George with me. He'll make a good apprentice."

"A princess?" Nancy asked, laughing.

"No, silly—a helper for Papa while I learn surveying. May I please?" George beamed at Momma, wide-eyed.

There had been no chin rub or glance toward Momma for approval. I breathed shallow and stared. She grabbed the fence again. Papa reached to steady her, but she pushed his hand away, shaking her head. After a deep sigh, she opened tear-filled eyes toward George and nodded.

"Yippie." He leapt to his feet.

My jaw dropped. *She's not thinking straight. It's too dangerous.*

Papa kissed Momma's cheek. "We'll get everything ready, then come for lunch. I have some news to share before we leave."

George matched Papa's stride on the way to the barn, and I followed Momma into the cabin.

I wanted to go in search of William McGuire. Someone has to stop Papa. I moved toward the door, about to lunge outside, but Momma's voice caught me.

"Did you hear me?"

With a gulp, I turned around.

"Take these to George." She held out a neatly folded new shirt and extra breeches.

It was the linen shirt I'd helped stitch. I took the clothes and scowled. "But he's too young. How can you let him go?"

Her eyes glistened as she stood with a peaceful expression. "Comes a time of letting our sons learn to be men, and he's been yearning for it for some time. Now, go on."

She walked away, dabbing her eyes, and I sauntered to the barn, mulling over her words.

Through the sun-streaked haze in the back corner, Papa was hoisting his transit onto Gideon's back. George stood at General's flank, securing a saddlebag, but jumped backward as I neared.

"Whew, you scared me, sneaking up like that."

I smiled and held out the garments. "Momma wants you to take these."

He frowned and stepped toward me. I flinched. The top of his head had never reached my chin before. *When did that happen?*

He whispered in my ear. "If we don't make it back, you have to be brave and take care of Momma."

I balled my fist, wanting to punch him. "Why would you say something like that?"

Holding a finger over his lips, he tilted his head toward the yard and grabbed the two wooded canteens, then handed me one. I followed him and General to the spring and squatted beside him.

Water gurgled into the canteen as he spoke. "Papa told me there are hostile Cherokee near Wood's Fort. He didn't want to worry Momma, but said we'd have to stay alert." George's eyes were big as he searched mine. "Slug me and tell me to be strong."

I shook my head and put my arms around him. "Hit me first. I can't believe he's taking you."

George pulled back and stood as Katie walked up.

"Lunch is ready. What's wrong?" She frowned.

I rose, smiling. "Nothing."

"But your eyes are watering."

I faked a sneeze. "Hay always bothers me."

"What hay?" Her eyebrows raised. She flipped her braid and pranced back to the shady tree, where our food waited.

I sighed and punched George's arm. "Be strong and courageous, Brother. I love you. Papa will keep you safe."

He nodded and shoved my shoulder. "Thanks. You too."

Papa passed us on his way to the shade. "Let's eat."

George shoveled in his last bite of diced carrots, and sat back, wiggling his leg, waiting. Papa took a final sip of coffee, released a quiet belch, and looked at Momma.

She pushed her plate away.

"When I get back from this survey in two weeks, we'll finalize preparations to leave. I received news a few weeks ago that Boonesborough is ready for settlement. If we meet Daniel Boone at his home on the Clinch River by the twenty-fifth of August, we can travel with his group. We'll have to leave here by the eighteenth, though." He looked at Momma. "If we don't go by then, I'll have to head to the Point and risk being drafted into a Continental regiment."

A sudden realization that he could be killed in the war made my legs go weak. *Did I want him to fight British troops or just be willing to?*

Momma pulled George into her arms.

He wiggled free, smiling. "I'll be all right. Don't worry."

"No use telling me not to worry. Now get." She gave his rear a playful swat, then reached around Papa's chest. "We'll start on the tobacco harvest while you're gone." Her eyes glistened as she gazed at Papa. "Bring my son home alive." She rushed from his arms and grabbed Charlie's and Sally's hands on her way inside the cabin.

After hugging George and Papa, I took the scrap bowl to the chickens and waited until the tinkling of survey equipment had faded before returning to the cabin.

Momma held a basketful of green pea pods in her lap and popped them open as the youngest children swarmed around her, holding up their palms. She gave each a handful. "Now, skedaddle."

I chuckled as they swirled like a whirlwind back into the yard to play.

Katie and Lizzy were sitting at the table, opening pods. I grabbed a handful and joined them in snacking on tangy peas.

Momma smiled. "You may each have one more handful. We need the rest for the stew. I've been sitting here assessing our tasks for the next two weeks. We'll lay out tobacco leaves each morning, then collect them once they're thoroughly moist. We need more waterproofed bags to keep our food dry, and we must make more bullets. One day next week, we'll scour the floor of the cabin with lye soap and sand."

I sneered. "Why go to all that trouble? We keep a clean home. And besides, the new people will be blessed enough to acquire our nice things if we don't return in two years."

She clasped her fingers together on the table and smiled at me. "I wish to treat our leasing couple to a fresh-smelling clean home—the way we'd want to be treated."

"That's what I figured you'd say." I forced a grin.

"As for the rest of the afternoon, we'll start on moccasins. I need to stay busy, so I won't worry about George. Papa has a good supply of rawhide for soles next to the roll of leather in the barn."

With a sigh, I said, "Yes, ma'am." I hated having to wear new hard-soled moccasins. They were always uncomfortable until one's foot toughened, but shoes would protect our feet from sharp rocks and brambles as we traveled the rough-cut trails to Kentucky.

Moccasin-making required a lot of measuring, cutting, and punching holes with an awl before stitching. But the work passed pleasantly under the shade tree. My fingers were numb by the time I finished whip-stitching the heel of the last shoe for the day—Sally's first real moccasins.

Momma examined the completed shoes. "Good job, girls. Thank you." She sat on a log and called Sally. "Come try on your moccasins."

Sally toddled up to Momma, sat on the ground, and lifted her foot. They were a good fit, and she wiggled her feet, admiring them, then toddled across the yard giggling and babbling, "Shoo, shoo."

"I have to have them back now." Momma held out her hands.

Sally shook her head and dashed away. "No. My."

I scooped her up from behind. Sally whimpered in protest as Momma removed the shoes. She handed them to Lizzy, who sealed the moccasins with a thick layer of bear grease and placed them to dry with the others.

Momma stood, rubbing her belly. "I recommend wearing your new moccasins outside every day now. The more they're broke in before the trip, the fewer blisters you'll have. I need to rest a bit before supper."

Katie whisked in beside me. "Do you think she's all right?"

"Things must twinge now and then as the baby grows in her belly." I watched her jaw drop and added, "She hasn't told us yet, so don't say anything. But you remember how she was before Sally came." I started toward the cabin. "Bring in fresh water and help me make hoecakes."

"Another baby." Katie shook her head and went to the spring.

I stepped onto the porch with my belly fluttering and prayed, *Help Momma feel better soon.*

Chapter Fourteen

Yellowing tobacco leaves flapped above my head in the hot August breeze. I plucked the lower golden ones, sending them twirling to the ground behind me to absorb the morning dew, and hurried down the row. Light-headedness grew worse by the time I finished. I shouted to Katie and Lizzy, "I can't do any more. Feeling puny. It's time to go to the creek and wash off."

Something in the leaves could make us deathly sick if exposed too long, even though we kept our sleeves long and wore leather gloves. One or two rows seemed to be my limit, and we were only two weeks into August. Momma couldn't help anymore. She picked one row the first day and had to quit because she felt dizzy. From then on, she and the other children tended to the last of the garden, harvesting, packing the vegetables in waterproof bags.

I couldn't go to the creek anymore without remembering Charlie facedown, nearly drowning, and Adam's rescue of him. I stepped into the deeper water and emerged up to my neck. Katie and Lizzy did the same.

"Do you think Adam and Big Jim made it to Williamsburg?" Katie went up the bank, wringing out her petticoat. "I've been wanting to ask Papa if he heard any news of them. But then, I'm afraid to know."

Lizzy bobbed up and down in the water. "I hope so."

"I prefer to imagine them well-fed and happy. No reason to ask otherwise. Let's get home." I hoisted my skirt above my knees and passed Katie so she wouldn't see tears pooling in my eyes. My real thoughts were that they had been caught or died on the way from lack. I shook my head and sighed.

As we came into the yard, Momma rose from the shade tree, holding her belly but smiling. "Eat a bite, then get the dents from the barn and make bullets. I'm going inside to rest. We'll get the tobacco bundled and hung in the shed later." Charlie and Sally toddled in behind her.

"Yes, ma'am," I said. *When is she going to tell us about the baby?*

I sat under the tree and nibbled on a hoecake while Susie and Nancy played nearby with clothespins as people.

Katie sighed. "Guess we're going to be doing all the work 'fore long."

"I reckon. Are you finished eating? Let's get started." I stood.

I brought the heavy container of dented bullets from the barn and sat it on the ground in front of the fire pit, and Katie stepped up with the molds.

Lizzy finished her last bite and came to help. "Can I melt and pour?"

"No. Let Mary do it." Katie set the bullet molds on a hot stone in the fire pit. "If you get burned, Momma will have to get up and tend to you. She's not feeling well."

"What's wrong with her?" Lizzy looked at me.

I cut my eyes at Katie before glancing at Lizzy. "You can't say anything, but she's going to have a baby. This one will be born in Kentucky."

"That's what I was wondering." Her tone startled Susie and Nancy, then she whispered, "Seems I remembered her being sick before Sally."

"You better not tell anyone. I mean it." I dropped a handful of lead dents into the cast-iron ladle and melted them over the coals. Holding my breath, I poured the hot liquid into warmed bullet molds as fast as I could without spilling or splattering.

It only took a few seconds for bullets to form, then Lizzy dumped them onto a cloth to dry and harden. I allowed Lizzy to help ease the cooled bullets into leather bullet pouches. "Always pour slow. Dented bullets won't fire straight."

Momma emerged with Charlie and Sally, looking refreshed. "Thank you for the bullets. Shall we get the tobacco in the shed?"

Once the leaves were bundled, five at a time with hemp twine, we tossed them into the wheelbarrow and carts. Inside the shed, the leaves were draped over wooden racks, which Katie and I hoisted by pulley ropes to the ceiling to dry. Dizziness forced me to sit on the grass outside and lay my head on raised knees. After a few deep breaths, I heard someone throw up behind some bushes.

Katie and Lizzy were sitting near me, and the others were playing chase. Poor Momma. Her face looked gaunt. "I'm glad Papa will be home to take over soon. I can't handle any more of these leaves." She staggered toward us and sat, inhaling deeply.

Drummer cocked his head and pounced toward the south road, sniffing the air and wagging his tail.

"Speak of the—" Momma chuckled and rose to her feet, shielding her eyes with the brim of her bonnet. "Thank the Lord; my son is in one piece."

Papa waved as he and George rode past us toward the barn. "Be out to help soon as we tend to the horses."

George grinned at Momma before lowering his head and slouching.

Momma frowned as she wobbled to her feet. I rushed to steady her and held her arm on the way to the cabin.

My siblings raced past us with the carts and wheelbarrow rattling with tools, before disappearing into the barn.

"What do you need help with?" I asked.

"Strength for the days ahead." She released my arm, then stooped, kissed my cheek, and smiled. "We need to draw rinse water for everyone's clothes and finish with supper."

"Yes, ma'am. I'll get the kettle filled."

I hugged Papa as he emerged from the barn but stepped back to speak. "We've finished today's tobacco harvest. There is only a half-acre left. But it's a strong batch, and it's making us sick."

"Fine job." He nodded, but looked serious. "How is Momma?"

I shook my head. "Not good. And she insisted on helping in the field. When will our new sibling arrive?"

Papa sighed, and his jaw clenched. "Not rightly sure. But Momma's not ready to mention it to the others yet." He took my hands. "Here's something else I don't want the others knowing. Not even Momma. George knows, because he heard it said to me from a man at Wood's Fort." His eyes studied me, which made my heart race. "Big Jim's body was found floating in the New River. Adam must have made it. I'm sorry. I wanted you to know so you can help George deal with it. He took it hard, and I know he likes to talk to you about his troubles."

Heaving sobs erupted as he wrapped me in his arms again. I pushed him away and ran into the woods. Stepping behind a juniper bush, I threw up, then sat back on the leaves and finished crying. If we had bought them, they wouldn't have run. Adam must have been devastated to have to continue without him. *Poor Big Jim. How frightened he must have been.* I sniffed and fumed all the way to the spring. After splashing water on my face, I filled the wash kettle and sauntered into the cabin to change.

George sat at the table with his head down. When I tapped his shoulder, his head barely raised. "I'm tired."

I leaned down and kissed the top of his head, whispering, "Glad you're home and not scalped."

His slight grin acknowledged me before he resumed his reclusive position.

After changing, I carried everyone's tobacco-soaked clothes to the kettle and used a stick to submerge them. They would soak until wash day.

"Time to eat," Katie said from the door. I joined everyone at the table.

Papa's mood was solemn as he bowed his head. "Thank you for provisions and safety. Give us good health, strength, and wisdom for the days to come." He fell silent. I glanced at him, but his head remained bowed. He cleared his throat. "Amen."

George's head bobbed because he fell asleep while sitting. When I snickered, he woke, looking around.

Papa smiled at Momma. "George was a good helper. He's learned his calculations well. Made me proud."

"He's a bit too pecked, though." Momma frowned. "What has exhausted him so?"

George took one bite of roasted rabbit and lowered his fork. "I'm not hungry. May I be excused?"

Momma nodded.

As he scooted back, he almost toppled from the chair, then hoisted himself up the ladder. I had to look away to keep my eyes from watering. *He really is distraught over Big Jim. Maybe he'll feel like talking tomorrow.*

Papa seemed pensive and ate only a few bites before sitting back to sip his coffee. "Too troubled by events to eat."

Momma wiped her mouth with a napkin and folded her hands in her lap.

I looked toward the ceiling and sighed.

"While speaking with the man I surveyed for, a letter arrived from his cousin in Boston. Sadly, his uncle, along with over a hundred provincial troops, were killed in a skirmish with His Majesty's Navy back in June. These men had tried to defend the city from a hill above, but the Regulars stormed up. The provincials forced the troops back twice, but ammunitions ran out during the third attack. No mercy was given." He shifted in his chair, clenching his jaw. "The man's cousin has joined the newly formed Continental Army, under the command of our own General Washington. He put out a call for riflemen a month ago, and a large company of Virginians are en route to Cambridge. There's no turning back."

I leaned forward, searching his face, waiting for him to say he was joining.

Papa sighed and took Momma's hand. "I must deliver important documents to Fort Cook before tomorrow night. I'll leave before dawn, ride hard, and make it back before dusk. God will understand my forsaking Sunday this time. It's important. We'll leave for Kentucky next Monday."

A seething breath rushed from my chest. Nausea swirled in my belly. I scooted away from the table and stepped onto the porch. When I sat, Drummer wagged his tail and plopped down beside me with his head in my lap. I rubbed his neck.

"Seven days. Our lives here are over because Papa's a traitor."

Chapter Fifteen

A moan from the privacy corner in the middle of the night woke me to a foul odor in the loft. The explosive sound indicated a bad flux. I hurried to open the shutter for fresh air and glanced at my siblings' pallets in the moonlight. George was missing. I tiptoed to the curtain and whispered, "Do you need Momma?"

He groaned again with another round.

"Who is that?" Katie asked.

"George is sick. I'm going to get another bucket and tell Momma."

Katie sat up. "Smells awful. I hope it isn't contagious."

"Me too." I moved to the ladder and caught a whiff of the same foulness emanating from his pallet.

The same smell swirled in the air below, even with the door opened to the night breeze and moonlight. Susie popped her head up. "Papa's got the flux. Momma went to the spring for water."

Fear gripped my stomach as I lighted the candle lantern and hung it on a hook from the rafter. *Whole families have died from the bloody flux.*

"George needs help." Katie rushed down the ladder before him.

He barely made it to the porch before leaving a trail of putrid diarrhea as he ran into the woods.

"Papa is sick too," I said. "Momma's with him somewhere. We need to get the wash kettles heating."

At that moment, Momma lugged a sloshing bucket onto the porch and set it down. "We need rags and more clean buckets of water. Papa and George are sick."

Katie glanced at me in the flickering light as if she had no idea what to do first. With a deep sigh and a head shake, I lifted the slop bucket from the peg beside the cabinet and carried the lantern toward the ladder. "Light another candle. I'll take this to Lizzy and bring George's bedding down."

"All right. I'll get the rags. Should we wake Susie and Nancy to help?"

"I'm awake." Suzie stood, rolling her pallet against the wall. "I'll get Nancy to help me fetch water for the kettles."

Shadows danced from the beams as I hung the lantern from a peg and whispered, "Gotta get up, Lizzy. There's sickness in the cabin. George soiled the loft. I'm taking his pallet down, but you'll need to empty the chamber pot. Here's a bucket for the overflow." I set it down beside her.

She whined, then gagged and sat up.

I went to the window for a deep breath, held it, and then scooped George's gooey pallet into my arms. I shivered with the willies all the way down the ladder.

"Whew." Nancy waved her hand in front of her nose as I carried the pallet past her and outside.

A blue-gray haze shone through the tall oaks around me. Leaves swished under my bare feet in the woods to a place downwind where I shook the soiled straw, tumbling it to the ground. I dragged the sheets and blankets back into the yard, spread them among some shrubs, then went to the spring for rinse water.

Momma approached with an apron-full of what smelled like primrose flowers. "Papa wants to speak with you. He's in the privy, but you can stand behind it and hear him through the wall. I'm going to make a remedy. They're not contagious—just ate raw fish for their breakfast yesterday. Thank the Lord they will recover in a few days. I'll send someone to take your place."

I set the bucket down, feeling panicked. *What could he want?*

Embarrassed, I eased behind the privy. "I'm here, Papa."

"I'm sorry to speak to you from here. There's a beaver-skinned pouch of sealed documents in that box in the loft that must reach Fort Cook by this evening. You're the only one that can go in my place. Wait." Papa moaned.

How can he ask this of me? I wanted to run away.

"Are you there?" He sounded raspy.

"Yes. But why can't they wait until you're well?"

"Must stop—No. I can't tell you. You'll be in more danger if you know. Wait." His bowels ran again.

My neck pulsed and breathing became labored. "I'm sorry you're sick, Papa, but I can't— No, I won't do this. I won't be a traitor like you."

Before he could say more, I dashed away from the privy. *I'm loyal to the patriots, not the loyalists.* Tears pooled, but I took a deep breath and wiped my eyes before entering the rank-smelling cabin.

Katie stepped onto the porch with a bowl of batter. "Momma said it's light enough outside to start making pancakes."

I sidestepped her on my way in.

"What was the secret?" Momma peered at me from the back privacy corner, where she was making two pallets.

"He wants those documents delivered to Fort Cook. I can't believe he's expecting me to go by myself—overnight."

"Stir the petals, please." She sounded irritated. "I need to check on George and Papa." She collected two clean blankets and rushed out the door.

The spicy scent of the steaming flowers calmed me. I lifted the spoon to my lips but cringed as I swallowed the thick salty-sweet syrup. Momma had added more salt than honey.

"Come on, Nancy." Susie spilled water on the porch, then knelt down to scrub George's trail with soap.

Momma will talk sense into him. I stirred and fumed. His willingness to sacrifice me for his cause crushed my chest. *How can he be so crass?*

Noise near Momma and Papa's bed meant Sally and Charlie were waking up. Charlie squatted in front of his pallet and attempted to roll it.

Sally toddled toward the door. "Momma?"

"I'm here, baby girl. Step back." Momma entered, helping George inside. He was wrapped in one of the gray wool blankets. He trembled with wet hair but had been scrubbed clean. "I made pallets for you and Papa over there next to the curtain."

I rushed past them and smoothed the covers. George lay down, and I covered him. "I hope you feel better soon."

Momma sighed and wiped tears from her cheek before dipping some of the primrose water into a cup. She turned toward the door, mumbling, "That man is bound and determined to kill himself getting to Fort Cook."

My breath caught. "He's going?"

At that moment, Papa entered, holding his gut, doubled over.

"At least drink this." Momma handed him the cup.

He sat in the chair, sipped, then grimaced as he swallowed. Momma stepped beside him. "Please don't do this. You'll tumble from you horse and lay there exposed all night. And for what—a parcel of documents?"

The cup trembled in his hand as he placed it on the table. "These are critical. Lives are counting on me. I'm sorry. I'll go slow and tie myself on."

"Nonsense. I'll go with you," Momma said. "Mary can take care of things here until we get back."

My gut wrenched. Big Jim came to mind. He and Adam could have escaped the night Adam pleaded with him too, but he deemed loyalty to Papa more important than his freedom. My eyes watered. *Is loyalty to the patriot cause more important than loyalty to my Papa?* I swallowed hard and threw my arms around his neck. "No, Papa. The family needs you. I'll go."

Papa whispered something in Momma's ear. She nodded, then rushed to me, pulling me into a hug with tears streaming down her cheeks. "Land sakes, I can't believe I've agreed to this, but you must pass yourself off as George."

Flabbergasted, I wondered how I could possibly pull it off with my soft voice and developing breasts.

She gathered a hunting shirt and two pairs of breeches from her mending basket. "I'll modify Papa's old hunting shirt while you try on these breeches. At least your hair is already platted like George's. Let's be quick before I come to my senses."

Momma led us up the ladder to the loft in spite of the lingering smell. I stayed near the window. The sun had risen above the horizon, casting golden beams through the open window, but not bright enough for sewing. She relighted the candle in the lantern.

I removed my petticoat and chemise, still in shock. Momma wrapped strips of linen around my chest, snug enough to flatten all protrusions.

"Raise your arms." She turned the shirt inside out and slipped it over my head, then quickly basted along the side seams. "Should hold overnight well enough. Now the pants."

George's pants were at least an inch too small around my hips. Momma shook her head and laughed as she held out Papa's. I slipped my legs in but had to hold them up to my waist while she cut and sewed.

"There's time to make Papa new ones," she said.

The breeches were still a bit baggy when she finished, but the shirt worked fine. Momma held her hand over her mouth. "Mercy me. What are we doing?"

"Don't worry, Momma. I'll stay out of sight and be safe. I promise." At least I *sounded* confident.

She took a deep breath, pulling me into her arms again, and my eyes watered. *How does George prevent tears?* I squeezed my eyes closed, then blinked several times.

My sisters gasped as I came around the curtain, and Charlie giggled. I removed George's hat from the peg and placed it on my head. "It's a good fit." I grinned at George, who rallied a glance before lying down again with a moan.

Papa rolled to his right side and motioned for me with his left hand. "Come sit here so I can talk to you."

I knelt down, kissed his stubbled cheek, and sat cross-legged on the floor. He stretched his left arm toward me, and I held his dry tanned hand. Papa grimaced and closed his eyes, releasing a foul-smelling fart under his blanket. I squeezed his hand in sympathy.

His eyes opened as he huffed out a breath. "I'm sorry this falls to you. The world is in chaos, but these dispatches will save many lives in the western settlements."

Loyalist lives. I stared through him.

"You may run into men along the way who'll ask where you're off to. Tell them, 'Fort Cook to mill corn.' They'll probably make you dismount and check the saddlebags, so fill them full." He took a deep breath. "They'll want to know your name, so don't forget to use George's. They might be looking for someone named Cage. But since you don't know who he is, you'll be safe to say so. They should let you go on your way."

His words seemed to bounce away from me before I could understand them. I focused on his mouth as he continued.

"Take the compass from my survey pack. You'll also need my hunting knife and bedroll. Along with the documents in the loft is a map. Follow the instructions on it to the drop location. Slide the pouch under your saddle and make sure it doesn't show. Do you understand?"

My head nodded in spite of an inner voice whining, *No.*

Papa's eyes glistened. "Follow the Indian Creek trail around the bend. You'll cross some creek branches, but none are deep. You should be able to make it in six hours. Wait at the forked tree on the map until dark. When you hear three taps on the tree from the courier, respond with two. Stay put until you hear the same three taps a little further away, then travel back to the bend and sleep. No matter what, stay away from Fort Cook." He shook his head and threw the covers back. "I can't let you do this. It's too dangerous."

I pushed his chest. "I'll be safer than you. Please lie back down and don't worry. I'm going." I kissed his cheek. He squeezed my hand, whispering, "Thank you."

George whispered, "Don't lose my hat." A faint grin rose from his pale lips.

"See you tomorrow." I smiled and stood.

Wide and teary-eyed siblings stood in a line, waiting to say goodbye. I knelt in front of the younger children, who took turns hugging my neck, but only Susie seemed to understand that I was doing something dangerous. "Stay safe," she said, kissing my cheek.

Tears streamed down Lizzy's face, and her voice trembled. "I love you, Mary. Please be extra careful. I'll be praying for you all day."

She squeezed me so hard, I squeaked, "I love you too."

Katie took my face in her hands and looked me in the eye. "You have to come back. I need you." She hugged me, then stepped back, turning away as she dabbed her eyes with her apron.

Momma shook her head and blew out a breath. "Keep your wits about you tonight and know that we are praying for you. Land sakes." Her eyes watered as she snuggled me in a long embrace. I lingered a moment, enjoying the crisp, fresh scent of the primrose petals she'd rubbed on her neck.

As I stepped back, Katie handed me the rifle. I shouldered it, then took the cartridge box from Lizzy and the powder horn from Susie. Momma gave me a knapsack full of hoecakes and jerky and turned away, sniffling.

My stomach fluttered as I picked up my hard-soled moccasins and stepped onto the porch, refusing to cry. I focused on each barefooted stride to the barn.

Streams of hazy yellow light filtered through cracks in the barn wall and illuminated glinting particles of dust, giving me hope of divine protection. "Be it fairies, angels, or from the throne of God himself—I'll take it."

Rebel whinnied as I laid my shoes on a barrel and approached him. "We have a scary trip to make, boy."

In one motion, I lifted the saddle pad from the rail and flung it onto his back. Standing on the stool, I heaved the saddle over him, but left it loose. "Be back in a minute."

My heart raced as I climbed into the loft and opened Papa's box. I picked up a thin tan pouch that had been sheared of all fur and coated with bear grease. Its flap was secured by a thin strip of sinew wrapped around a sewn-on sliver of bone but could be easily unwound. The paper-sleeved dispatches were sealed with beeswax and stamped *AL*.

After re-wrapping the documents, I removed the map and scurried back down. *No time to examine it now.* I slid the map and pouch under the saddle and cinched the straps.

Items needed to spend the night alone in the woods were packed as they came to my mind, including my moccasins. I secured Papa's bedroll, attached the scabbard to the saddle, then found his compass and hunting knife. I filled a waterproof canvas bag with enough oats to last Rebel two days and attached it to the saddlebags of corn. A separate bag contained a hoof pick and curry comb for grooming. Drummer whimpered at my feet. I knelt down and scratched him behind the ears. "Sorry, boy, I wish I could take you. Stay."

I double-checked Rebel's comfort, led him into the yard, and mounted. Wiggling into the saddle, I hoped to wake from a dream—ready to help Momma with breakfast. But my family clambered onto the porch waving.

Moving in a slow gait past them, I tipped my hat for practice and chuckled. Papa beamed and nodded, then hunched down, holding his belly as he went back inside with the others. My chest tightened.

The sun hadn't waited to rise midway through the trees, nor had the forest creatures. They scurried about, singing and chattering as if it were a normal day. *But here I am, risking my life to betray William McGuire tonight—at least I assume he's Papa's courier at the forked hickory tree I saw on his survey a while back.* I rubbed Rebel's neck and let tears and words flow freely as I recited Papa's instructions in my head, especially what to say if stopped. *I can't believe I'm doing this.*

As the forest swallowed me, I felt lonely. Fear became a knot in my stomach. Speaking aloud seemed the best remedy. "I'm alone for the first time in my life, pretending to be a boy, and tonight I'll be fending for myself in the dark, trying to sleep while all manner of wild creatures stalk me. Now why did I have to say that? Maybe silence is best." But I wanted to scream.

On my cue, Rebel sprinted up the eastern trail. *God, make me invisible.*

Chapter Sixteen

When the trail curved easterly after a half mile or so, Rebel snorted, and my good sense returned. I slowed him to a walk to cool him down before dismounting. "Sorry, boy." After loosening the cinch, I removed his bit and attached the rope to his halter before leading him to a grassy place in the shade. "Just needed to get away before I screamed like one of those Irish banshees Papa told me about." I chuckled. "Have you ever heard one? Papa said they sound just like a screeching barn owl that flew from the barn when I was six and sent me bawling to Momma." I stroked his neck. "We'll walk most of the day, I promise."

Rebel ripped a clump of grass from the ground with his teeth while I checked his feet, then I reached under the saddle and pulled out the map. "Let's take a look at this." Rebel ignored me as I sat beside him, unfolding the map as it flapped in the warm breeze.

Two light squiggly lines and one darker joined the double-lined Indian Creek diagram, indicating the creeks Papa had mentioned. "I hope these little crosses show where to ford." A few miles west of the small square was a forked tree with a circle at the base, marked with *CS*. "Just like that survey plat I found on my birthday. Now, what was the riddle?"

Rebel eased to the bank of the creek as I read the notation written under the diagram.

Seven miles to Hans Creek, then two miles to a forked tree marked CS.

"Well, boy, we better get going. It's already near nine of the clock." I folded the map and placed it back under the saddle. After tightening the cinch, I reached into my knapsack for a slice of jerky and ate my breakfast while giving the lead rope a gentle tug. Rebel followed me back to the trail. "Nine miles might be a half day for Papa, but it's going to take us longer. Don't know how the crossings will be or how rough the ridges. I might even have to wear my shoes."

The trail remained fairly level and allowed a quick pace, but the further from home I roamed, the more I grew aware of my smallness. I listened beyond the sound of our steps on the forest floor and the usual bird tweets or scurrying creatures rustling the leaves. My ears were tuned for the unusual crackling tree limbs, snapping twigs, or growls from daytime scavengers finishing breakfast. And, thanks to Papa, men on the lookout for someone named Cage. This evening I'd be sleeping with night predators stalking around. "You'll alert me to danger, won't you, boy?" To relieve my tizzy, I succumbed to humming the frog-courting tune.

After a northerly curve, the well-worn path led to a grassy clearing where our first intersecting creek, marked Fitz Run, required nothing more than an easy hop over. I lingered, allowing Rebel a drink and a short graze before clicking my cheek for him to come. So far, I had no use for my shoes, and our first two miles had taken an hour and a half.

It was a short distance to the next creek on the map: Red Sulphur Springs. Its strong smell seemed to draw Rebel to drink heartily. I scooped some in my palm and tasted but opted for the canteen of spring water from home, but the cold water refreshed my tired feet.

To my dismay, the terrain changed to rocky and steep within two and a half miles of changing to a southern course. I endured a few sharp jabs to my uncalloused arches, but pushed myself and Rebel to go a bit longer than two hours. At this level, Indian Creek ran ankle deep and made for a refreshing way to cool and soothe my throbbing feet. I watched minnows swarm around my ankles a minute before joining Rebel in the shade to eat and rest a bit.

"About three hours from here, boy. I'm ready to ride for a while." I pulled my shoes from the saddlebag with a sigh and slipped them on before mounting.

It was an easy two hours to a wide creek called Hans that followed the steep rocky ridges downward into a thick, dark forest. I dismounted and traversed along the ridgeline down to a trail leading across, which Papa had marked on the map. He had also marked the distance from our home as seven miles from here and almost two miles to the forked tree. "At least another hour." I squinted through the treetops for the sun's location and guessed the time to be two of the clock, or near enough.

Rebel and I were drenched in sweat when I led him into knee-deep water and stood in the middle, cooling off while he drank. He raised his head, sniffing the air, then snorted and bobbed his head. Holding my breath, I turned in the direction of a black bear lumbering down the steep bank. I exhaled slowly as my heart pounded. I took Rebel's reins to steady him.

The bear sniffed the air, growling low as it paced the bank, watching us. I stood still. *God, make it leave.* It stepped into the creek, observed us a moment, then proceeded along the opposite bank, fishing.

My heart pounded as I mustered a deep breath and a *thank-you* before backing slowly out of the water, leading Rebel. The bear rose on its hindquarters and lunged once with a grunt, watching us.

I slipped Rebel his bit and mounted, easing him away from the creek with my stomach churning. Deep breaths calmed me, but the reality of what could have been set me to crying and wishing I were home before I dried my face with my sleeve. *I don't know how to be a boy.*

Galloping for several minutes eased my mind enough to slow to a walk and realize that Rebel needed to graze. I made a thorough scan of the area before dismounting, but he seemed skittish and wouldn't leave me to search for plots of grass.

"I'll give you a little grain to tide you over. Should be foliage again once we rejoin Indian Creek." I secured the canvas bag over his nose, with the straps behind his ears, then dug into my knapsack for a slice of bear jerky and sat on a fallen log.

I took a bite and thought about how brave Katie had been. "Wish you were here to talk to. You'd understand my fear."

Rebel looked at me but kept chewing.

Loss of sleep, a full belly, and the heat of the afternoon made my eyes close several times, but fear of not waking before dark forced me to my feet. I knelt at the creek and splashed water on my face, allowing it to dribble down my shirt and through the stifling binding around my chest. "I have to stay alert." Shadowy figures seemed to dart in and out among the trees and made the hair on the back of my neck prickle.

"Delusions." I shook my head, took Rebel's lead rope, and headed up the ridge. "Or could be scouts from Fort Cook? We're within its perimeter. Besides, Indians would have jumped me by now to steal you. In either case, I better not cry anymore, and you really shouldn't worry so much."

Walking up the steep bank in wet moccasins rubbed a raw place on the ball of my right foot. On top of the ridge, I paused to catch my breath and remove the shoes. A throbbing blister had formed. Rebel nuzzled my hand, and I rubbed his neck. "Less than an hour; we'll be at the tree." Even saying it aloud refreshed me. "As soon as my hand is free of those dispatches, we'll find a place to shelter and rest. If I didn't have to wait for the signal after dark, we'd just make our way toward home. I sure wish you could talk." I stuffed the moccasins into the saddlebag and mounted.

As we rounded a slight curve back toward the east, I spotted a deep ravine with rock ledges and an area that might be hiding a cave. "If it's not occupied, maybe we can shelter there later."

A few more yards from the trail loomed a large old hickory tree with wide pear-shaped leaves and a forked trunk. My breaths shallowed as we approached. I stopped beside it, stared down, but couldn't move.

"We're here, but I don't want to do this." I stuffed the map under the saddle, scanned the area, and took my time dismounting before stepping around to Rebel's head. I scratched his neck, then sighed and pulled the pouch from under the saddle.

My belly churned as I carried the foul thing to the tree. I examined the trunk and found the initials *CS*. At its base, a round blue-gray river stone lay among several flat gray stones. They would have appeared natural enough if I hadn't known its secret. The riddle came back to me. *A rolling stone gathers no moss.*

I squatted, removed the smaller rocks, and flipped over the round one. A layer of dried moss covered a rectangular tin box that was wrapped in otter skin, but it was empty. Wiping my hands on the front of my shirt, I sat cross-legged on the ground and stared at the tin while Rebel grazed nearby.

"If I don't do this, I'll have to tell Papa I did. But what if people die because I didn't? He'd be blamed. Then what?" I shook my head and rolled onto my knees with my gut wrenching. *Guilt—no matter what I do.*

I lowered the tan pouch inside, then swiped my hands together, cleansing them from the feel of it. After re-wrapping and covering the box exactly as it had been before, I dashed toward Rebel and grabbed his reins. He jerked his head.

"Sorry, boy. It's all right. Let's get back to the ravine and find a place to take a nap until dark."

As soon as we returned to the trail, two men strolled out of the woods within a rock's throw, pointing rifles at me. I stopped with a gasp.

A tall redheaded burly man shouted, "Who are you, lad?"

I went blank.

"State your name and business 'fore we beat you." An older dark-haired man scowled, and spit tobacco juice on the ground.

"George...Shirley." I made my voice deep, but my teeth chattered.

"Aye. And where ya be headed?" The tall man stepped closer.

"Taking corn to be milled." I pointed to the saddlebags, breathing shallow. *What if they find my map?*

"Well, tarnation, boy. Ain't you headed the wrong direction?" The older man spat again and approached Rebel. "Let's jest see what ye got in here." He flipped each of the bags open and nodded to the other man. "Seems to check out." He pointed his finger toward the road behind me and glared. "The fort is this-a-way, same place we're headed. So, you might as well accompany us."

They seem suspicious of me. What if they're the ones Papa warned me about? "I need to relieve myself first." I crossed my legs the way George always did when he needed to pee.

"Well, dad-blame-it, hurry up. We ain't got all day. Vittles are waitin' at the fort."

I ran to a crop of bushes, actually needing to pee. They laughed and turned away, examining Rebel. *At least they're allowing me privacy. Now what? Papa told me to stay away from the fort. I can't risk being questioned or discovered as a girl. They already think I'm a loyalist spy.*

After securing my breeches, I sneaked down the ravine and found a large oak tree with a hollow trunk. I picked up an arm's-length stick and stirred it around the inside. When nothing growled or came out, I squeezed myself in—willing myself not to cry. *They might find the map and the document, but they won't find me. My heart raced. But what if they take Rebel and all my supplies?*

"Where'd you go, lad?" the taller man hollered.

"Tarnation, boy." The older man sounded angry. "Have you been et by a bear, or are ye just a cowardly loyalist?" The leaves shuffled in my direction. "We seen you come down this-a-way. Why you hiding?" He sounded close. "Reckon you don't have no more need of that fine gelding then."

"Leave him be, Reese," the other man shouted. "We'll report him to the captain and flip for the horse. Hope you're not a loyalist, lad. If a bear gnaws on your lousy flesh in the night, it's sure to die 'fore morning." He and the older man laughed.

In spite of leaves rustling back up the ridge, I stayed still inside my tree and prayed. *Please, don't let them take Rebel.*

Falling forward woke me in time to land on my forearms and not my face. I stayed on my belly, scanning the area, disoriented by the darkening forest and gray clouds. *What time is it?* I brushed stick and rock debris from my skinned arms, then crawled up the ridge and peeked over. Sickened by Rebel's absence, I laid my head on folded arms and cried until George's voice in my head said, "Be strong," followed by Momma saying, "Keep your wits about you."

I sniffled once more and sat up. To the right of me lay a rotted log. Papa made me eat a grub when I was eight, so I wouldn't be afraid to. He said they were a good meat and water source. With a sigh, I rolled the log over, plucked one off the wood, and quickly swallowed the dirt-flavored lump before gagging.

"I'll look for plants in the morning. Better check the cave for shelter first, then find a spring." Speaking aloud helped stifle my fear and loneliness, but not my agony over Rebel. How could those men leave me stranded without my horse, supplies, and rifle? How can they be so evil? "I want my horse back," I yelled to God.

Once down the hill, I searched for a long, broken branch with a sharp point. Holding it like a bayonet, I crept round the rocky crags along a fading footpath that led through a low-lying cave entrance. *Please be unoccupied.* I picked up a rock and threw it inside to test for depth. It thudded against stone.

When nothing attacked, swarmed, or growled, I shuffled into the dank shallow cavern and glanced at an old leaf bed, indicating previous use. The lack of fresh claw marks confirmed its availability. *Sufficient for one night.*

I crawled from the cave, still grieving for Rebel and all my supplies. "Guess those men thought I'd come to my senses and follow them to Fort Cook." *Maybe they'll come back.*

Following an overgrown section of the trail past the cave, I spotted a trickle of water flowing down a limestone wall. I curled my tongue into a trough and stuck it to the rock with my head tilted back, swallowing enough gritty, sweet wetness to be refreshed.

I made my way back to the hickory tree, noting the path back to the cave before hunkering down in a clump of nearby shrubs. I leaned my back against an oak tree and awaited the secret taps.

Night birds, crickets, and frogs serenaded. A distant wolf howled. But when an owl hooted a few trees over, my breath caught. *Why fear banshees in the night when real wildlife is scary enough?* A gust of wind rattled the tree limbs, and thunder rumbled from distant western ridges. *Why didn't I go to the fort with those men?*

Chapter Seventeen

As I waited in the shrubs near the hickory tree, clouds swept across the full moon and crackled with jagged streaks of lightning, but I hoped they would blow cross the Blue Ridge Mountains before accumulating into a storm.

Barks and yelps from what sounded like hundreds of coyotes erupted from the woods all around until they moved on. Then it happened—three distinct raps on the hickory. I hit the oak next to me twice and listened.

A slight rustle of leaves, the cue of a turtledove, then someone shoved me to the ground face first. A knee dug into my back, holding me down.

"And who would you be?" The man's slight Irish accent sounded irritated.

Unable to breathe or wiggle free, I spat moldy leaves and dirt from my mouth but didn't answer.

The knee released from my back. Squeezing me together at my arms, he lifted me to my feet, then wrapped an arm around my neck, preventing me from turning my head to look at him.

I writhed and shouted, "Let go of me."

"Be still." His voice softened, but his grip remained firm. "What's your business out here?"

Not knowing if he was friend or foe, I said nothing.

"Why did you respond to my tapping, George Shirley?"

He knows my name! Too scared to respond, I swallowed.

He sighed in my ear and cleared his throat. "The men that took your horse are scouts from the fort. They were waiting to give your papa a message, but you confounded things by escaping. Taking your horse and supplies was meant to force you to the fort for questioning. I recognized the sorrel as Michael Shirley's. Where is he?"

His voice sounded familiar somehow, and the explanation made sense, but how would he have seen Rebel before...unless...*William McGuire himself?* I sucked in a breath but refrained from spilling the truth and what I knew about Papa. *What if this man is a loyalist spy trying to trap me?*

"He's too sick to come. He told me to respond to the taps and not to go to the fort. Where's my horse? I have to get home in the morning."

"Stay still and listen." He released me, then darted behind a tree before I could see him or move. "You're in danger because of these dispatches. Tories between here and the New River are watching for Cage. They've discovered he's a turncoat and are seeking his identity, but they don't know he's your papa."

I gasped. *Papa's a patriot?*

"You can't go home the way you came. A loyalist spy reported a lone rider headed toward Hans Creek. Now they're waiting in ambush."

His words made me shudder. *That's why I thought someone was watching me.*

"You and your horse don't match the description of Cage, but it'll be safer to take the main road back to Indian Creek. Your horse and supplies are on the other side of the forked tree."

I fought the desire to squeal with joy and remembered to be George. "Thank you for getting him back, sir." I wanted to ask him a hundred questions, but he spoke first.

"Hunker down in someone's barn. There's a storm heading in tonight. Best for you not to be seen, like your papa said. How old are you, anyway?"

I couldn't say eight because of my size, and if this was William, he might have seen George before and would know he wasn't thirteen.

"Well, you're mighty brave, George Shirley." His hand stuck out from behind the tree.

I shook it and deepened my voice. "Why are the dispatches so important?"

He cleared his throat. "They confirm loyalists in this area who are involved with Connelly and Dunmore, who are recruiting a large force of Indians to attack the western settlements from the fort at Detroit. Forces under Colonel Lewis and General Clark are working toward defense, but in a few days, these loyalists will know your papa betrayed them as Cage. Tell him I said, 'God's speed to Kentucky.'"

"What is your name, sir?" My heart raced.

"He'll know. Wait for me to strike the tree three times before you come for your horse."

Disappointed by his non-answer, I fished with different bait. "How did you know he belongs to my papa?"

No answer, only the sound of leaves rustling away and a distant rumble of thunder. *Had to be William. How else would he know Rebel belongs to Papa?*

I waited in the hazy moonlight until the distant raps ended, then rushed to find Rebel. "I'm sorry, boy. I'm so glad to have you back." I embraced him, weeping.

"Let's get to the cave. The storm is getting closer. Why find a barn to sleep in along the road when there is a perfectly good cave?"

I stumbled over large rocks and roots in the dark, leading Rebel to the cave. I removed his bridle and bit, then secured his rope to the closest tree branch. I pulled my tinderbox from my knapsack and lighted a candle with my flint stone. I dripped wax onto a rock, planted the flickering candle in it, and groomed Rebel while he munched on grain from his feed sack. My thoughts raced with all the news William McGuire gave me. "All this time, Papa has been gathering information against the loyalists instead of being one! But he said he would remain loyal. When did he change his mind? Did he lie?" I sighed and carried the saddle and all supplies inside.

The horse pad added extra cushion under my bedroll. I removed George's hat and set it on the ground beside me, and used the saddle as a pillow.

An explosion of thunder caused me to bolt straight up. My head cracked on the low rock ceiling before pain laid me down, moaning and trying not to pass out. I felt a knot swelling, but no wetness from blood. It took a few minutes to recover my senses and remember where I was and why.

Rain fell in a torrent, and wind whipped through the trees. Limbs cracked and crashed down around the cave. I feared for Rebel, but there was nothing I could do. Water poured into the cave and accumulated without draining, making the reason for its abandonment clear. I was in danger of drowning. I forced George's hat over my swollen head, tossed everything out into the flooding ravine, and threw the soggy pad over Rebel. He pranced sideways and shook with a snort. "I'm sorry to startle you. Be still now. We have to go." I heaved the saddle onto his back along with the loose bedroll and bags. I shouldered the gun and powder horn, then put the headstall on him. I untied and tugged on the rope, and Rebel and I struggled up the slippery bank to the ridge in a downpour.

"That's why William said to find a barn. Why didn't I listen?"

On top of the ridge, I tightened the cinch, mounted, and headed toward the road, holding on to George's hat with both hands in the gusty wind, trusting Rebel's eyesight as rain stung my eyes and skin. When the jagged outline of the fort's picket walls loomed ahead, I wanted to go in but veered to the south, along the road I'd seen on the map marked Cook's Run. I rubbed Rebel's neck and shouted over the rumble of thunder, "Maybe there will be a barn soon. We'll have to wait till morning to head home."

Images of Momma standing on the porch with the lantern held out into the darkness made me cry. But I drew strength knowing my family would be praying for me on account of this storm.

Within an hour, the storm slacked off, and broken clouds allowed occasional peeks of moonlight. I halted and dismounted. "How are you doing, boy?" I ran my hands down the length of his legs, checking for swelling. He seemed fine. I scratched his neck and hugged him. "We've had a rough night. Good boy." I dug into the drenched grain bag and offered him a handful, which he accepted.

I pulled out a cloth of soggy jerky and ate several bites. The more I moved around, the more the side of my head pounded. I removed the hat and touched an egg-sized knot. "We can't go on like this."

After scanning the horizon for any sign of a barn or settler's home, I led Rebel off the road. "Let's just find a high flat place and lie down. I'm getting dizzy."

We walked up a bank and found an area that would work for the night. I unsaddled, and spread the gear, grain, and jerky out to dry. Cuddling Papa's blanket, I lay on the soggy horse pad.

As I drifted to sleep, a voice yelled, "I think he's up there." Startled, I sat up glancing around, but no one was there.

Chapter Eighteen

"Stop it. My head hurts." I waved my arm, trying to push George away, but it was Rebel nudging my shoulder. I sat up, squinting. "All right, I'm awake."

The tantalizing aroma of bacon frying made me smile. "Someone is cooking breakfast nearby. No wonder I thought I was at home. The sudden remembrance of the voice from last night unnerved me. "We better stay quiet."

My legs wobbled as I stood and walked to the blanket where the grain was spread. I scooped handfuls into the feedbag and let Rebel eat his fill. "Best get all you want this morning. I'll have to throw the rest to the birds." The growl in my belly soon outweighed the warning not to be seen. "Soon as you're done, we'll find the source of that bacon. Maybe some kind soul will have pity on a lone boy with soggy jerky. Then we'll head off alone again."

While Rebel ate, I checked the corn in the saddlebags, amazed that most of it was dry. Everything else was still wet. I shook out the blankets and rolled them before repacking.

"Sorry, boy, I'm going to have to use the soggy pad, but I won't ride unless desperate."

His head bobbed when the heavier pad slapped his back, but he resumed chewing while I saddled and cinched. After relieving his nose of the feedbag, I scratched him behind the ears. "Good boy. Soon as we get home, I'll give you a good rubdown. "Let's get going." I took the rope and led him toward the whiff of bacon.

Two men were camped on the other side of the road. They dressed as men from a township, not in common hunting shirts like men from here. One stood upon seeing me and waved. "Morning. Come on down if you have a hankering. Coffee's hot."

Caution gave way to the additional lure of fresh ground coffee—and company. *If they're traveling toward the New River, maybe they'll allow us to join them. We'll be less noticeable with companions since the loyalists are looking for a single rider.*

We eased down the hill. "Thank you for the invitation. The storm about ruined my supplies." I made my voice sound deep and held out my hand in greeting. "Name's George."

"Welcome." The man who invited me down shook my hand as I stopped in front of him. His caramel-colored hair was tied back with a black ribbon, and he wore his beaver-skin hat, side-folded with a brass rosette, but his eyelids slanted downward, giving him an unattractive droopy look. "Name's Jinks. What happened to you?" He smiled and stared at my forehead.

"Busted my head on a rock when the storm jolted me awake." I ignored their curious stares. They didn't need to know I'd sheltered in a shallow cave down in a ravine with a storm coming.

Jinks shook his head. "Terrible storm, for sure. Tributaries all along the Indian are flooded."

The other man stood from the frying pan and came toward me, holding out his hand. His clothing, though similar to Jinks's, was unkempt and his dark hair untidy. Leaving Rebel to graze, I stepped forward to shake his hand.

"We were at the narrows on Hans Creek yesterdee bear huntin'. Name's Toloman. Have a sit down."

I glared at his neck and froze; sure he was wearing the neckerchief I'd given to Adam. There were gold initials and green leaves visible in the right corner. My heart raced as I bit my lips to keep from asking where he got it and what happened to Adam. Papa said that Big Jim had drowned, but Adam had gotten away. I took a deep breath to calm down before looking him in the eye.

Toloman's face turned red. He took the neckerchief off and stuffed it in his knapsack. "I know'd it looked too frilly with all those swirls. Didn't want that runaway Negro to keep it neither."

"Sorry for staring." My voice quavered as I looked at my feet, hiding my watering eyes, then swallowed and faced him. "Looks like the one my sister made. A slave by the name of Adam took it before he escaped." *Half true.* "If the initials are MS, she'd want it back."

He nodded and handed it to me. "Sure. Ain't no use in me looking like a dang fool wearing it."

Fighting tears was torturous as I held the precious item in my hand. "What happened to the runaway?" I stuffed the neckerchief in the front of my shirt and pretended not to care.

"Sold off to West Indies traders. We chased him and another to the New River crossing on Rich Creek back in May. The other one drown. Dang shame too—he would have fetched near a thousand pounds."

My stomach churned as I nodded and sighed. "But why not return him to his master?"

Toloman leaned his head back, laughing. "Don't be naïve, boy. Too valuable to waste when a profit can be made."

Anger churned in my stomach as Jinks handed me a cup of coffee.

"Thank you." I sucked in a deep breath and took a sip of the bitter brew.

Toloman offered me a plate of bacon and hoecakes. "Where you headed?"

"Toward Indian Creek." I took the plate, but my appetite was gone. I lied without flinching. "Had business at Cook's yesterday." Weariness pressed on my shoulders from sorrow, and the pounding in my head came from the hat pressing on my swollen temple.

"You're welcome to travel with us to the junction. Best not travel alone these days. Never know who's friend or foe."

I took a bite of bacon and sipped coffee while I thought about his offer. "I'd be grateful." *They seem friendly enough.*

Toloman sat on a large rock beside me. "Eat up then."

Jinks wiped his mouth on the sleeve of his shirt. "Who's your pa?"

"Michael Shirley on Indian Creek." I pretended to sip the sludge in my cup, hoping he and George were recovered. "Where're you going?"

"We have business in Williamsburg." Jinks dumped the coffee grounds and began packing. "Long trip ahead. Are you ready?"

"Yes, sir." I emptied the cup and handed it to Jinks on my way to Rebel.

After packing the neckerchief in my knapsack, I double-checked the horse's legs and hooves.

"Fine-looking horse. You race him?" Toloman asked.

"Naw." I smiled. "He's fast though."

Toloman tightened the cinch of his saddle and peered at me. "Well, now, if I had something to wager, I'd challenge that claim."

"Tarnation, Tol. You lost to William McGuire the other day, and this horse looks to be his equal."

I smiled and bragged, "My papa bought this horse from Mr. McGuire."

They looked at each other, then glared at me, frowning.

My breath caught. *Why are they looking at me that way?* I mounted and would have bolted, but Toloman laughed.

"Just my luck," he said on his way back to his horse.

Jinks shrugged, smiled at me, and mounted, but I worried over their reaction and stayed behind them, keeping to a leisurely pace to avoid saying any more.

In a few minutes, Jinks veered off the road, motioning for me to follow.

I halted and shook my head. "I'll take my leave and stick to the road. Thank you for breakfast."

"Go on thataway if you've a mind to, but this trail is quicker. Come or don't." Toloman smirked.

Jinks rode up beside me. "Don't trust us? If we wanted to waylay you, boy, we would've by now." He laughed. "Come on with us. Don't waste time staying on the road."

What if they are telling the truth? Fear of being alone prompted me to reconsider.

"Come on, Tol. We ain't got time to coddle this boy." Jinks rode on, and Toloman left.

I took a deep breath and followed.

A few minutes into the forest, Jinks gave a shrill whistle, and four men emerged from behind trees.

As my heart skipped a beat, Toloman's foot shoved me off Rebel. I landed hard on the ground and pain shot through my right shoulder as if it jammed. Someone grabbed my left arm and jerked me to my feet. I cradled my injured arm, groaning as my stomach churned.

The man beside me slapped my face. "Shut up, boy."

"Who is this?" A man stormed toward me, dressed in a ruffled white linen shirt with a tri-fold black hat. His breeches were blue with a red stripe on the sides.

The contents of my belly rose into my chest.

Toloman glared at me. "This here is the son of Cage, Captain, sir. Confirmed this morning at breakfast. Said his pa is Michael Shirley on Indian Creek."

Bile rose to my throat. *I gave Papa away.* With a coughing heave, I threw up on the man who confined me. He shoved me to the ground, cursing, and kicked me in the ribs twice before someone intervened. Moaning and crying, I rose to my knees before spewing again. I struggled to stop crying as Jinks handed Rebel's rope to the man and continued the conversation in front of me. *They're going to kill me, then go after Papa.*

"The boy confirmed William McGuire's association with Cage. Said his pa bought this horse from him. Scouts came into the fort yesterday, bragging how they took it from a scared loyalist boy west of the fort. McGuire took the horse and went out to investigate."

Tears burned in my eyes. *I've endangered William too. God save my family and the McGuires. Help me be strong.*

"Stand up, boy. Stop that blubbering 'fore I give you something to whimper about. Did you deliver a dispatch to William McGuire last night?"

Glaring at the man, I swallowed bile and staggered to my feet.

"Don't you be defiant, boy." The captain got in my face, raising his hand as if to slap me, but his foul a breath made me gag. He backed up, turning toward a group of men, yelling something in a language I didn't understand.

A near-naked Indian, painted red with black zigzagged lines, rushed toward me with venomous dark eyes, snarling with a scalping knife raised above his head. I squatted to the ground, unable to breathe as I hunched into a ball with my eyes closed, expecting a deathblow.

"I'm only going to ask you one more time." The captain snatched George's hat from my head. "Did you deliver a dispatch?"

"Hey, that ain't no boy.," someone shouted. "I seen her with her pa at Fort Culbertson a few months back."

I sucked in air and glanced up at the man with a two-inch scar on his left cheek.

"Remember ol' Isaiah Brown, sweet thing?" He squatted in front of me, grinning, then spit tobacco juice beside my foot.

Isaiah moved aside as the captain stepped up. "What the—?" He grabbed my left arm and lifted me to my feet, glowering at my chest. "Bound up tighter than a drum. Stand up here—let's take a look." He reached for the buttons on my shirt as if he'd become a wild beast, tearing at me and licking his lips. But Momma's strong threads held. My heart pounded as I jerked away, but he grabbed my braid, and Isaiah grabbed me from behind me.

As I screamed, "No," shots erupted all around.

The men turned away and scrambled to their rifles.

My ears crackled as I rushed to Rebel and pulled him into the woods with my chest pounding. Searing pain from my rib cage made breathing hard. *I can do this.* I found a stump, gritted my teeth, and hoisted my leg over him. Cringing as my right shoulder tensed, I took the reins in my left hand. "Go!" I kicked his flanks hard, and we fled west, following the creek as a volley of gunfire erupted behind us. Breaths heaved and tears streamed from my eyes, making it hard to see. *Help, God. I must make it home to warn Papa.*

Rebel carried me with surefooted speed along the trail until I slowed him to a walk. His nostrils flared with labored breaths. "Sorry, boy. A little farther, then we'll hide and rest a minute. I don't know where we are. I have to think." My body trembled, and a weakness I'd never felt before came over me. "I must be in shock." *Please, don't let me die.*

Chapter Nineteen

I headed north along the creek, ducking under tree limbs and trusting Rebel to find a trail. When the way became too brambled, I slid off, breathing through the pain, and pulled out the hunting knife. I hacked through the tangle, barely feeling the pricks and scratches to my arms and face, until too weak to make one more swipe. I removed my rifle from the scabbard with my good arm and slung the powder onto my shoulder. I loosened the saddle and removed the bit, then walked away from Rebel, needing to relieve myself. Afterward, I climbed up a ridge and found a place to rest behind some bushes that allowed a clear aim in case anyone had followed. Rebel drank from the creek and found grass.

All was quiet except for my stomach growling. I glanced around at the vegetation around me and rolled a log over. I worked up a good amount of saliva, popped a gritty grub into my mouth, and gulped it down, followed by another. *Need to stay strong.*

My eyelids grew heavy, but I forced myself to keep scanning. Rebel looked toward the brambles from which we came. I rose to my right knee and checked the powder in the pan before steading the rifle against my throbbing right shoulder. Bracing my left elbow on my left thigh, I steadied my right arm, took aim, and waited to see what would emerge.

Isaiah slunk through the bushes holding up a hatchet and eased closer to Rebel. He stopped and glanced around. I wanted to blow his head off. *But first I need to know where I am and how far to Indian Creek.*

"Come on out, girl. I won't hurt you. It's just you and me now. The others are dead or captured. Shot up by men from Cooks. I'll take you to your pa."

No, you won't. You're about to be wounded. I watched to see if anyone else lurked around. The only movement came from his horse, nipping at the grass in the bushes.

"You hear me? Don't be scared. You don't want to be out here after dark, injured and all. The wild critters will eat you. I won't hurt you—I promise." He shrugged, then reached for Rebel's rope and led him back toward the bushes.

My breath caught. *No you don't.* Ignoring the pain, I aimed for his kneecap and fired.

His holler echoed from the steep banks as he writhed on the ground, spewing curses I'd never heard before. Rebel lunged across the creek in a panic.

That should slow you down. I reloaded and made myself breathe. My heart raced as I watched.

Isaiah removed his neckerchief and wrapped it around his leg as he yelled more curses. "Dad-blame-it, girl. What's wrong with you? You're meaner than the Devil himself. Least I know you're alive. Don't leave me here like this."

When no one came out of the woods to see about him. I took a deep breath, rose from the bush, and scooted down the ridge on my rear, holding the gun on him as I glared. "Don't move."

His eyes held fear as he nodded.

"Throw that hatchet in the creek and any other weapons. Tell me what creek this is, or I'll shoot your other knee and leave you to the scavengers."

His hatchet splashed in the water, then he removed a hunting knife and tossed it in. "My gun was took. That's why I tore out of there. This is Hans Creek." He held his leg, grimacing and rocking.

I pointed the barrel at his other leg. "How many miles to Indian Creek from here?"

His eyes widened. "A mile or so, north." He pointed. "Please, fetch my horse and let me get to Fort Cook for help?"

After working up a mouthful of saliva, I spit in his face. "Fetch it yourself." I slammed the butt of my gun down on his bloody knee and stepped toward Rebel as the vile man wailed.

"Come, boy." When Rebel trotted back to me, I sheathed my rifle, then hugged his neck, crying.

Isaiah stopped cursing long enough to yell, "I'm going to kill you, girl."

Fear knotted in my gut. *I'm I going to have to kill him. What if he finds his weapons and makes it to his horse?* A voice in my head said, *Ignore him. He'll have to get to Fort Cook before bleeding to death.*

I blew out a breath to calm my nerves and led Rebel to a fallen tree before mounting. We headed north in a quick trot.

A glimpse at the sun above the treetops indicated it was near noon. "At least five hours to home with a slow pace." *But I'm exhausted and injured.* I want to be home now," I screamed. "We'll get to the mouth of the creek, find a hiding place, and rest for a while."

The narrow trail descended the ridge, through thickening forest, and into the scariest darkness I'd ever seen in the middle of the day. Ancient trees, as wide as I was tall, allowed only a glimmer of light, but it was an excruciating ride down with my jammed shoulder. The trail wound around rock walls with crags and openings to caves of unknown size. Signs of fresh claw marks, scat, and a musky scent energized me to move faster, in spite of mind-numbing pain. "This is a bear habitat, boy. We've got to get away from here quick. What if Isaiah lied and we're headed the wrong way? May he rot in Hades if he lied."

When I came to a tall rock ledge, I dismounted and pulled the compass from the knapsack. It was difficult to see, but the needle still pointed north. When I took a step forward, my foot slipped on a pile of mud. I landed hard on my rear and dropped my gun. Searing pain shot through my shoulder and up my back. I sat there bawling, smelling like puke, and with a new blister throbbing on the ball of my foot.

But a stench emanated beyond my own. I looked at the ground near my foot. It wasn't mud I'd slipped in but fresh bear scat. *Gotta get out of here.* My heart raced as I grabbed a stick and used it like a crutch to stand. I pulled the blanket from Rebel and managed to tie two corners together for a makeshift sling.

Rebel suddenly bolted back up the embankment before I could call him back. A growl preceded a large black bear emerging from one of the caves between us. Rebel raced away, and the bear lumbered his direction. I swallowed hard and took the opportunity to run in the opposite direction toward Indian Creek. A vision of Papa jumping to his feet shouting "*Oui-shi-cat-to-oui*" propelled me forward as if someone pushed me from behind.

When I paused to catch my breath and looked back, nothing was chasing me. My chest felt crushed as I bawled and worried about Rebel. *He's fast. He'll get away. Someone will find him if he makes it back to the road.* I sat on my rear, sniffling and praying that he'd find a kind new owner. I glanced around, knowing it was time to get out of this horrible abyss and make it home somehow.

After what seemed like an hour, daylight burst from a clearing, and my stomach fluttered with hope. Indian Creek shimmered with silvery splashes as it tumbled over rocks. I wanted to plop down in the middle of it, soothe my achy body, and the inflamed blister on my foot. But my greater need was to get away from Hans Creek and find a safe place to rest and treat my wounds.

With each step, I cringed in pain but focused on fixed points ahead, until I recognized one of my previous resting places. I plunged into the cold water, washing the dried puke from my shirt, then found a hole deep enough to sit in. The cold water soothed my ribs, pulsing shoulder, and the now ruptured blister. I leaned back, staring into the sky, and felt myself floating past glowing clouds and into the endless blue. Fear of drowning in the middle of Indian Creek snapped me out of my stupor.

My body ached all over as I rose, then hobbled along the bank, collecting a few plantain leaves. I found a dry place to sit, eased my foot from its shoe, and placed crushed leaves against the oozing blister. With a deep breath, I gritted my teeth and slipped my moccasin back on, allowing myself to cry as I stood there.

How am I going to make it four more hours on this foot?

My first steps were agonizing, but searching the area led to a small willow tree growing near the bank. I found a sharp stone and hacked at the bark until I could peel the outer layer away. I managed to dig out a few moist fibers to chew. Tongue-numbing juice tingled down my throat and instantly eased my headache. *Maybe it will dull the pain raging through my body.*

Another glance around revealed an overhanging rock behind a grove of sycamore trees. *Perfect.* I made my way there and squatted, curling up my knees. I leaned against the wall and closed my eyes. *Just a short nap, and I can make it home.*

The late-afternoon heat made me nauseated as I woke, but my body refused to move. I turned away from the rock wall, stretched out my legs, then scooted away on my rear. The pain from my shoulder and ribs made standing excruciating. But my foot seemed better. *Must get home to Momma before dark.*

I made my right foot move, followed by my left, all the way to the creek. I splashed water on my head and neck and drank as much as I could.

The creek had flooded the banks in some areas, and the soggy ground made sucking noises as I slogged through the bogs. My only company was the squirrels rushing up the tall tree trunks. Occasionally, one would scurry along a branch and chatter at me. Blue jays screeched, and finches flitted and chirped among the shrubs as I staggered along worrying. First about Rebel, then I worried that Isaiah had blabbed to loyalists about William McGuire's involvement with Papa. *Maybe I should have gone to the fort. What if William's been captured? I've got to get home and tell Papa so he can warn him.*

Chapter Twenty

Time slipped by uncounted until the sun slipped below the tree line, and I reached Red Sulphur Springs. "My family will be preparing supper soon." Weak and parched, I lay on my belly, gulped the odorous water, and ingested some of the soft gritty clay for the minerals. I sat up and eased my swollen foot into the water without removing the moccasin, afraid I wouldn't be able to put it back on. I hoped the mineral water would be a good remedy.

Two more hours. I sighed. My body ached, and heat radiated all over me in spite of soaking my feet. Two images on horseback seemed to sway toward me. A shiver went up my back. I didn't know if they were real. To be safe, I reached for my rifle but couldn't find it, then remembered I had lost it when Rebel ran. *Nothing I can do.*

Someone shouted in Papa's voice, "I'm here, polliwog. I'll get you home."

Gentle arms wrapped around me, and Papa peered into my eyes. "I'm sorry this has happened. Put your arms around my neck. I'm going to lift you."

It seemed to be a dream until he stood with me. Agonizing pain caused me to moan as he swooped me up and carried me to Little Sis. "Swing your leg over."

I straddled the horse and took a deep breath, shivering as Papa mounted behind me, holding me to his chest. I whispered, "I love you, Papa. I'm sorry."

"Shh, we'll talk later."

The other man rode away before I could make out who he was. Papa urged Little Sis into a canter. The jolt made me whine.

"I know it hurts, baby girl. Hang on."

I wept in his arms. *I did it. I'm alive and going home.*

Drummer's yapping lifted my head from Papa's chest. I squinted at the two-story log home and my family pouring into the yard, first with smiles, then with frowns and sniffles. But joy flitted in my stomach. *Thank you, God. I don't know how or why I'm alive.*

I gasped from the pain of Papa leaning me forward as he dismounted.

"Slide down slow, and I'll carry you inside." His arms were raised toward me.

Sucking in a breath, I lifted my leg and cringed with the twisting motion that propelled me from Little Sis into Papa's grasp as I groaned.

He whisked me onto the porch and past Momma, who said, "Take her to the table."

I shook my head. "I'm not hungry."

Momma chuckled. "It's easier for me to reach your wounds from the table."

Papa laid me on the table gently and placed his arms around me with tears streaming down his cheeks. "Thank you, God, for the return of our precious daughter. Please heal her quickly."

I grabbed Papa's shirt and peered at him. "The loyalists know who you are, and now, they know William is involved. It's my fault. I—"

"Let me in here." Momma nudged Papa out of the way as she hugged my head and kissed my cheek. "I need to tend to her now. Tell Katie and Lizzy to bring the water and plants. The rest of the children need to stay outside until I get Mary settled." Her hand was cold as she felt my forehead and cheeks. "You're feverish. Where are your wounds?"

I swallowed and whispered, "Foot, ribs, shoulder, and head. But I need to talk to Papa."

"Shh, we'll talk later." Papa wiped his face with his sleeve.

Momma kissed my forehead, then untied my blanket sling. "I'm going to undress you and give you a sponge bath while I assess your wounds."

I nodded and cradled my arm to prevent it from dropping too fast. Tears fell. "Thank you, Momma."

When the binding around my chest dropped away, fresh air filled my lungs so fast I felt dizzy. Momma gasped and stroked my left side. "Land sakes. Bad bruising, but I don't think the ribs are broken." Leaning her ear against me, she said, "Take a deep breath."

I sucked in air as the door opened. My good arm instinctively covered my exposed chest as Katie entered with an apron-full of something. Lizzy came in and set the water bucket on the counter. Katie smiled at me, then closed and latched the door behind her.

Momma stood straight and addressed them. "Put half of the willow shaving in the water to soak and the rest in the broth to simmer."

"Yes, ma'am," Katie said.

Momma squatted back down to my side. "Again."

I breathed in and out until she moved away and sighed. "Sounds clear." She glanced at Lizzy. "Mary needs a cup of water and bring me the lye soap." She felt along the collarbone, holding my elbow as she moved my arm and watched my face. When I grimaced, she felt the bone again. "Thank the Lord. I didn't feel any separations. I think everything is just jammed. When I get you cleaned up and dressed, Papa can adjust your arm."

I widened my eyes at her.

She nodded. "It will hurt, but we want it to heal proper." She stepped behind me and unbraided what remained braided of my hair. "What a mess," she said, shaking her head.

Lizzy lifted the top of my hand to her lips, kissing it before giving me the wooden cup. "I'm so happy you're home alive."

I smiled with watering eyes. "Me too."

"I'm going to wash your back first," Momma said, but the sudden gush of cold spring water down my back caught my breath as I jerked.

Momma laughed. "I'm sorry, but heating the water will take too long, and the cool water will lower your fever. Besides, you're smelling up the cabin."

She scrubbed and rinsed me all the way around, then held a blanket up while I washed my private parts. After wrapping the blanket around my shoulders, she snuggled me, and I laid my head on her shoulder. I would have fallen asleep, but she moved. "Lie back down now, and I'll see about your feet."

"Bad blister on my right. I think it's festered." I stretched my legs out on the table.

Katie helped me to my back, placing a straw-stuffed pillow behind my head. She kissed my cheek and hugged my head. "I love you. I'm glad you made it home. I've been praying hard."

I screamed and raised up to bolt when Momma removed my moccasin. She held her breath and peeled away the blood-soaked leaves. "This is serious."

The room grew dark, and comprehension left me.

My foot stung as if hundreds of yellow jackets had attacked. I shook it and tried to run, but Papa leaned over me, holding me down on the table.

"Shh, be still. Momma has to kill the infection with turpentine and honey. Look at me." He stroked my hair and smiled. "Mr. McGuire told us you were missing when he found Rebel and brought him home. He helped me find you." Papa's voice cracked as I cringed.

Tears wet my cheeks as the reality of Papa's words sank in. I smiled. "Rebel's home?"

"He's resting in the barn."

Sudden vivid images flooded my mind. I took a deep breath and began to tell what had happened. "It was horrible—"

Searing pain shot up my leg as Momma scraped my foot, then applied more of the tincture that burned like the blazes while I moaned. She wrapped my foot in strips of linen and kissed my forehead. "That's all for now. I'll have to do this again in the morning. We'll move you to a pallet on the floor next to Susie."

"At least I adjusted your arm while you were passed out." Papa grinned and helped me sit up before he moved out of the way.

My shoulder didn't feel jammed anymore, but still hurt.

Katie held up a dry privacy blanket, and Momma slipped a clean chemise on me before wrapping me in another blanket. "Now, Papa can help you to the pallet, but bend your knee, and don't place your foot on the floor. I'll bring a cup of willow broth."

I swung my legs around and scooted as Papa lifted. "One hop at a time." Papa grinned.

I smiled before taking a deep breath. "I'm sorry I didn't listen to you about staying out of sight. Even Will...Mr. McGuire told me not to be seen. He was the man at the forked tree, wasn't he?"

Papa nodded and smiled. I held Papa's arm and hopped to the pallet, where he eased me down and sat beside me, stroking my hair. "Least the ruse of being a boy worked. Mr. McGuire said he had no idea. Said the man you shot in the knee rode into Fort Cook hollering about a being shot by an Indian. William knew the man had been with the ones captured in the woods and confronted him. He confessed the truth and said you rode down Hans Creek, headed home." Papa wiped his face. "I'm sorry." His voice trembled.

I reached for his hand. "I'm proud of you, Papa, and everything you've done to expose those men and their plan against settlements in the west. We need to leave for Kentucky—quick. Mr. McGuire said the loyalists will come for you. We're all in danger." My eyes watered. "William now too. I mean, Mr. McGuire."

Papa sighed and took my hand to his lips. "He told me."

I glanced around the too-quiet cabin. "Where are the littles and George?"

"Taking care of chores and playing," Papa said.

My breath caught. "They're not in the woods, are they?"

"No. They've been instructed to stay close."

"I want to tell what happened while they're outside." I decided to start with meeting those men at breakfast. "I need my knapsack."

Papa placed his arm under my armpits and lifted me in one motion, which seemed to be the least painful way.

Katie brought me the bag, and she and Lizzy sat on the floor.

Momma peeked out the shutter before bringing a steaming cup and lowering the handle into my hand. She caressed my back and sat beside Papa, cuddling his arm.

"Thank you." I closed my eyes, slurping the warm salty broth and savoring it in my mouth before swallowing. I handed the cup back to Momma with my eyes watering and pulled my neckerchief from the knapsack. "This was on the neck of one of the traitors this morning." I showed my initials. "It's the one I gave to Adam." My breaths heaved as I held the cloth to my chest. "He was captured and sold to traders leaving for the West Indies." I frowned at Papa. "Adam thought Governor Dunmore would give him freedom for escaping."

Papa sighed and shook his head. "It's a lie. Most are sold at great profits to fund the king's troops."

Grief bowed my head. "How can they be so cruel?" I sniffled.

"How did you get it back?" Katie dabbed her eyes with her apron.

I took a deep breath and laid the neckerchief in my lap. "Told them the slave stole it from my sister and that she'd want it back. The man had no more use of it. They were friendly, and I thought it would be safe to travel with them."

Reliving the account while I told it stirred the same emotions as when it had happened. I had to stop several times and sip my broth. The worst retelling came with the moment Isaiah Brown recognized me and told the others I was a girl. "They were vile men and would have violated me."

Momma held her hand over her mouth, and stares from my sisters widened. Papa stood, holding his belly, and I lowered my head before facing them again. "But thanks be to God, gunfire erupted, allowing me time to escape with Rebel."

"Enough." Momma stood, wiping her face. "Drink the rest of this broth. It's time for you to rest while we get supper on the table and see about the children. Probably getting into mischief by now."

My sisters followed her.

Papa helped me lie back. His eyes glistened. "Scouts at the fort alerted the captain that known traitors looking for Cage were nearby. One mentioned that the boy, seen the night before, was with them. They rounded up some men to remedy the situation and bring you back. But when the skirmish ended, you weren't there."

He kissed my forehead. "My brave daughter."

"When did you change your mind about being a loyalist? I read the letter from Colonel Preston, commending you for being loyal and to follow British survey laws and about the McGuire's being patriots."

Papa grinned. "Seems I remember saying that you didn't understand everything. But you need to know Colonel Preston isn't a loyalist, and survey filing had to wait on officials to confirm the changes." He leaned to my ear and whispered, "I've been on the patriot side since January, but I couldn't say so."

"Oh, Papa!" I sat up and wrapped my arms around his neck. "I should have trusted you. I should have never snooped into your affairs and thought evil of you. I've been so wrong and so worried. I love you. I'm relieved you're not a loyalist. I'm sorry. I promise to trust you for the rest of my life, even if I don't understand."

He rocked me and hummed the German lullaby as the cabin resumed the sounds of normal life, with my younger siblings entering.

"You may greet Mary, but don't touch her. She has injuries," Papa said as he helped me lie back.

Four of them squatted beside me at the same time, grinning but not talking.

I smiled. "I'll be better in a few days."

"What are enginries?" Nancy asked.

"Hurts." Susie glanced at her before leaning close enough to kiss my forehead. Nancy, Charlie, and Sally followed suit, then scooted away, giggling.

George sat down beside me, whispering, "I heard Mr. McGuire tell Papa everything. It pained me to hear, and I never saw Papa break down weeping before. I was scared for you. Glad you made it."

I reached for his hand, and he took hold. "I'm sorry I lost your hat. Is Rebel all right? He was chased by a big black bear."

He nodded. "There was a skinned place, but Mr. McGuire had already tended to it when he brought him."

George giggled. "I was standing there when he told Papa, 'George is missing.' Don't worry about the hat. It was getting tight anyway. Papa said he'd get me a new one at Fort Culbertson before we leave."

George squeezed my hand and went to the table before I could ask how William reacted to me being a girl. But I imagined his jaw dropping and him feeling bad for shoving me to the ground at the forked tree. *Shame I can't tell him not to fret.* I smiled and rolled to my side as Papa bowed his head and prayed.

"Thank you for the safe return of Mary. Help her wounds to heal quickly. Thank you for the abundance of our harvest, and may it sustain us on our journey to Kentucky."

My belly fluttered at the mention. But after what I'd been through alone, the trip to Kentucky with my family didn't seem daunting at all. Papa had said it's good, fertile land. There will be other families, maybe girls my age, and fearless men protecting the western settlements.

I glanced at my gold and green initials on the neckerchief made for my first dance and shoved it under my straw stuffed pillow. *Best not to dream too far into the future until this dang war is over.*

Papa's soothing voice drew me back. "We ask for your protection from harm and wisdom in the days to come. Amen."

As the family passed bowls of carrots, potatoes, and a platter of sliced meat around the table, my stomach growled. I stood, then hobbled to the table before Momma could protest, and plopped on the bench beside Katie, out of breath. "What's on the platter?"

"Turkey." George beamed. "We heard one gobble in the woods this morning."

"Perfect. Last things I ate were grubs."

My siblings echoed, "Ew."

I laughed. So far, my thirteenth year had been difficult, but my family had become more dear to me. We were all stronger. No matter what lay ahead of us in Kentucky, I knew we'd get through it together.

Acknowledgments

Hugs to my patient family for supporting me as I followed my dream but challenged me not to neglect them. Thank you to the multitudes who encouraged me along this journey.

To those who critiqued my early versions and told me it was good with straight faces—but saw my potential.

Special thanks to C. S. Lakin for professional critiques, edits, and guidance since 2008.

In memory of my publisher friend, Evelyn M. Byrne-Kusch, who produced the first editions of the first three books of this series.

A huge thank you in memory of my uncle, James Warner Earwood, who kept the family history, and, in whose records, I discovered Mary and her family, the inspiration for this historical fiction series.

About Author

Phyllis A. Still is living her dream as an award-winning author in Texas. She is an eighth-generation descendant of DAR Patriot, Mary Shirley McGuire, the inspiration behind the *Dangerous Loyalties* series. Phyllis loves her family, pets, road trips, history, and playing games with her grandchildren. Her adventurous childhood through seven states created her vivid imagination and a love for stories about people who have overcome hardships.

I love hearing from my readers. Please consider leaving a review online at Barnes & Noble, Amazon, Goodreads, or your favorite book source. Join my Dangerous Loyalties Series fan group on Facebook. Learn more about me at phyllisastill.com

Ready to learn what happens next?

Fleeing the Shadows

Dangerous Loyalties, Book Two

Fleeing the Shadows is a stirring, nail-biter of a read and will be sure to please fans of the first book of the series….the story rips right off the page…for a historical YA novel, Still does not hold back on making sure that we feel the desperation of the family in every chapter…Still has a great YA voice that carries the reader away with her pages. **—Literary Titan**

Wholly enjoyable, and quite intense and shocking at times…this is a historical series to take note of and one I definitely want to keep following. **—The Miramichi Reader**

2017 Literary Titan Five Star Award Winner

Fleeing the Shadows, Book Two in the Dangerous Loyalties Series inspired by Daughters of the American Revolution Patriot Mary Shirley McGuire.

Kentucky Territory, 1775: Pitted against the dangers of the wilderness and things lurking in the shadows, thirteen-year-old Mary Shirley and her family must flee Indian Creek ahead of those seeking to hang her papa as a spy.

The perilous trip to the Boonesborough settlement is further complicated by her momma expecting a baby. Mary is determined to be strong and not complain as she and her seven younger siblings endure steep rocky paths, thick, dark forests, and vile frontier men.

After a disastrous attack leaves them stranded and Papa wounded, Mary once again must risk her life, push through pain and fear, seeking fort scouts before the shadows of death overtake her family.